D0917257

THE DEVIL'S TRENCH

LUCAS PEDERSON

SEVERED PRESS
HOBART TASMANIA

THE DEVIL'S TRENCH

Copyright © 2019 Lucas Pederson
Copyright © 2019 by Severed Press

WWW.SEVEREDPRESS.COM

All rights reserved. No part of this book may be
reproduced or transmitted in any form or by any
electronic or mechanical means, including
photocopying, recording or by any information and
retrieval system, without the written permission of
the publisher and author, except where permitted by law.
This novel is a work of fiction. Names,
characters, places and incidents are the product of
the author's imagination, or are used fictitiously.
Any resemblance to actual events, locales or persons,
living or dead, is purely coincidental.

ISBN: 978-1-925840-59-9

All rights reserved.

DEDICATION

To my dear, beautiful mother, Theresa. You battled a monster, protecting us from our father, and now you battle a different monster with ALS. You are the embodiment of courage and I am forever proud to be your son. I love you, Mom. Always, and forever.

Because I feel that, in the Heavens above,
The angels, whispering to one another,
Can find, among their burning terms of love,
None so devotional as that of "Mother,"
Therefore by that dear name I long have called you—
You who are more than mother unto me,
And fill my heart of hearts, where Death installed you. –To My Mother

Edgar Allen Poe

CHAPTER 1

As happens, the tide rolls in, drowning all life in its wake.

The sky is old blood draining from a sour wound. Such blood, Ig Hawkins remembers well. A life she wishes to forget. But the ghosts of the past never stay dead. They never stop haunting…

She watches the tide rise over the rocky beach and fill Liar's Cove not far to the north and sucks in a quick puff from her inhaler. The waters won't reach her where she sits on the grassy area above the beach. But it'll be close. Close enough for what she needs.

Overhead, seagulls cry, searching for anything they can scavenge. Too bad for them, they won't find much. Not yet anyway.

Ig's gaze drifts out over the vast Pacific Ocean and wonders if Em is watching. And if she is…what does she think of Ig doing what she's about to do?

Doesn't matter.

Ig stands as the tides roll closer toward the grasses of the upper beach.

It's almost time.

She unhooks the mesh sack from her belt and readies herself.

An ancient secret handed down from her grandfather, Ig stares at the creeping tide. She stands, slightly hunched, legs apart, mesh bag dangling.

"Never trust the sea," her grandfather used to say. "It is the sea which cannot be claimed or ruled over. Ah, but her tides, Iggy…her tides bring great bounties if one pays attention."

And she does pay attention. Has for years.

Now—

Oh, hell, now is not the time to be thinking.

The tides roll up to the grasses. And when they recede a bit, she's left with what has always been in this region. One of the only incomes she's ever had. Though fewer and fewer as time goes on.

The milky pods stick to the sand as the waters slip away. Working quickly, she gathers the pods into the sack until it's full. She's finished before the tide returns, flooding the rest of the beach.

Ig backs up, hefting her harvest. An okay haul. Not great like it used to be, but it'll do.

She swings the sack over her shoulder as the small, translucent pods squirm and mewl.

***

"That's it?" Berkley shifts, wooden chair creaking at his considerable weight. He squints at the small haul with his remaining eye. "Ya got some dark ones too."

Ig rolls her eyes. "You know they're overharvested, Berk. A deal's a deal."

The fat, old man scratches near the empty socket of his left eye with the long nail of a chubby pinky finger. The elderly ship rocked sluggishly back and forth in a soothing rhythm to the waves.

Once upon a time, the old ship used to sail the oceans, Berkley its captain. Many years ago, right after Earth had enough of humanity's shit. It flipped and jumbled climates. Earthquakes broke everything. The super volcano under Yellow Stone exploded, laying waste to almost everything in America. The ash was enough to blot out the sun. Many died during that transition. Those who were able to avoid the fallout for years.

Not Ol' Berkley, though. He'd been riding the seas, hunting treasures said to be here or there buried by pirates, when the ocean surged and, as he tells it, a "real-life godsdamn Kraken" attacked his ship. His crew fought the thing, but not before one of the two-foot-thick tentacles bashed the side of Berk's face, knocking "m'eyeball right out its damn socket. Popped right out," Berk had said. "Clean as ya please. Had to cut the pink stingers with m'knife or that ol' eyeball would be just floppin' all over m'face." They managed to fight the "kraken" off, but it left the hull of the restored pirate ship with a hole that took in more water than they could bail out or fix.

Those who survived the attack escaped on lifeboats, including Berkley.

The next day he paid to have his ship resurrected and brought to Andi Docks where the hole was patched and the ship secured to the final dock. The one never used by fishermen. And there it remained, becoming a center of trade and sales hub for the Northern Pacific of the more…exotic.

Some called Berkley a thief. Some called him a conman. A fraud. Some called him a tycoon.

He's all of those to some degree, but not heartless.

Now, he fetches a sigh, picks the sack of elish pods up and plops it down on a scale. The digital numbers blink 5.6lbs.

Berkley grunts. "Things must not be spawnin' like they used to, eh?"

"They're dying off, Berk. Overfished, and we keep taking their offspring. What did you think would happen?"

Nodding, he pulls open a drawer in his desk, sifts around a bit, and tosses a banded stack of bills. "Rounded'er up to six pounds. That's ten." He gave Ig a very rare smile and tossed a smaller stack of bills next to the first one. "That's your severance pay."

"Severance pay?" Ig frowns at the old man. "You're firing me?"

He slides the money drawer shut and eases himself into the padded chair. "Lyvs are goin' extinct. Can't sell pods if there aren't any."

By lyvs, he means the strange reborn livyatan species that really isn't so much whale or fish, but something of both worlds. Instead of eggs or live birth, they spread fertilized pods.

"So, let them spawn. Let them rebuild their numbers again. I could gather something else. I could—"

"I'm shuttin' down, kid." He sighs, lowers his head a bit. "Getting' too old to be swimmin' with the sharks. Gonna pull up anchor and go south."

Ig opens her mouth, closes it.

His cheeks puff out with a breath. "I gave your name to an old friend. A very rich old friend. He should be contacting you for work."

Still not sure what to say, Ig nods. She picks up the stacks of money, turns to leave.

"I'm not finished, kid."

Ig stops and faces him for the last time. The ship rocks, groaning and creaking.

His haggard, grizzled face softens some, remaining eye shimmering in the pale light above the desk. "How long have you worked for me?"

"Ten years."

He nods. "Long time these days. Loyalty is a rare trait." His chubby fingers drum the desk for a moment. Then he yanks open the drawer again and tosses an even larger stack of bills at her. He lifts a quieting hand when she begins to protest. "Don't wanna hear it, kid. You've collected, harvested, and given me everythin' I asked for all ten years. Consider that compensation for loyalty."

"I...I don't know what to say."

He smiles, and for the first time (a night for firsts, apparently), it's almost grandfatherly. "No need to say anythin', kid. Thank you for all those years you had to deal with my sour ass. Now, go. My friend will be contactin' ya soon."

There feels like more should be said and she stands there trying to think of the right words for almost a minute.

Finally, she manages, "Thank you."

He smiles. "Get home, kid. Take care of yours. Don't ever stop being you."

She can't help but smile back at him. He gives a nod and she leaves the ship, never intending to set foot on it again.

The night is cool on her sweaty skin. It's always unusually hot in Berkley's ship. She stuffs the cash into her satchel and hurries away from the docks. With the beach and Berkley's ship at her back, she wades through tall grasses toward home.

The tall grasses aren't the safest of places, but it's faster than going around the mile-long swath of grass. She keeps her hand on the butt of her revolver. Things hide in the grasses, be it deranged humans…or something else. The world was never safe before the climate shifts, but now, mutated things stalk every region. Some are escaped lab experiments, others from unknown origins. People have become just as dangerous. As resources deplete, they're reduced to scavenging and pillaging. They group up into militias and form their own communities and the Government doesn't care. If it ever had in the first place, these days, they let America crumble while lining their big pockets with blood money.

America, in every sense of the word, has become an assassin nation. Killing and covering up and getting paid decently for it. Ig wouldn't be surprised when another power asks them to annihilate all of America. Commit genocide.

Such is surviving in America now.

A dark, foreboding hellscape in most regions east of what used to be the Rocky Mountains. Luckily, the West Coast, nothing but a narrow, tattered strip of land about forty miles wide and stretching seven hundred miles long, despite its dangers, is one of the better regions to live in. Earthquakes and rising sea levels about drowned the entire state during the climate shifts.

At least, with the climates finally switched and jumbling no more, everything has fallen into a strange kind of norm. For now, anyway. Who knows when the world will turn itself upside down and inside out again. But, until then, Ig has other, more important things to deal with.

Her heart sinks at the very thought, the weight of it all as she drags herself toward home.

***

Crickets and frogs do their nightly orchestra thing. Other than this and ocean waves at her back, the night is calm. Silent. Practically dead.

Ig steps out of the tall grasses and into a swamp. Nothing marshy. The ground is like walking on a sponge, but other than that, only a few pools of stagnant water here and there. The only thing bad thing about the swamp is the smell. Like wet, dead leaves and mud. Of something almost moldy. The dank and sour stench of decaying vegetation.

She walks the trail, scraggly trees soon closing in on either side. A swamp giving way to woods. Soon, the inky night sky with its sliver of moon disappears as the tree canopy thickens overhead. Always feels like she's walking through a large tunnel.

It awed her when she was young, and still does now.

The twists and snarls of the branches. The curves of the trunks. Shiny plants and sharp weeds swaying in a mild breeze. This is her safe place. Nothing bad has ever happened to her out here in the woods. This natural tunnel. It's more home than home, these days.

Eventually, the woods open to a small meadow and standing about center is a small, elderly house. Little more than a shack, really. Ah, but it's home.

Or, used to be anyway.

All the lights are off, as usual. No electricity out here.

Once, there had been a time when she'd emerge from the woods to find all the windows aglow in candlelight. On chilly nights, pale smoke would swirl from the chimney and the sweet smell of burning wood never failed to bring a smile to her face. Times back then weren't exactly simple or easy, or safe, but there seemed to be much more warmth and things to be happy about. Things to be grateful for. She's not sure what happened besides getting older and seeing the world with gradually jading eyes…or if her view of everything changed a year ago.

Perhaps both.

Ig, satchel full of bills, makes her way to her home.

She stops, forehead resting against the cool, splintery wood of the door. Her hands clench into tight, shaky fists for a moment, then relax. A long breath, too heavy to be a sigh, blows out of her.

"It's okay," she whispers to herself. "I'm okay."

Then she unlocks the door, and steps inside her house.

CHAPTER 2

"Wh-Who's there?"

Ig sighs, lights the entryway candle, and says, "It's me, Mom."

Beyond the flickering glow of the candle, the rest of the house rests in darkness.

"I...I can't get up."

Ig locks the door, moves into the dining room, and tosses her satchel on the table. She lights the candle there and sets about lighting the rest, saving her mom's bedroom for last. It's cold in here, but...first thing's first.

She lights the first candle inside Mom's doorway, begins to step inside, and backs away quickly, covering her mouth and nose with a trembling hand. She should be used to this by now, but every time she's running late...

"I—I'm sorry," Mom says, voice a whimper. "I couldn't make it to the...the...well whatever is it."

She means the bathroom or if not that, the bedpan. Her mind is drifting more and more each day. Doc Reynolds is still shocked she's made it this long. "Pure bullheaded will," Reynolds says.

Ig can attest to that, but also...in the spiritual sense of her ancestors...perhaps it's not time for Mom to go yet. There must be something more the woman is meant to do. Although, personally, Ig can't figure out what that could be.

She steals herself and enters the room, lighting every candle so the small space connected to the bathroom is bright enough to bite back the shadows.

Here, she pauses, staring at a candle flame, back to her mom.

"How...how was your day, honey?"

Fighting tears, Ig nods. "Okay. Well, I don't know. Lost my job."

"Wh-What? I thought...I don't know. Sorry. I'm so sorry."

Her words come out mushy and slurred, but, at least comprehensible. Ig dreads the day when Mom can no longer speak, nor swallow. And that day is coming. Ig just tries not to dwell on it too much.

Finally, she faces her mother. The only one left of her family. Once she's gone, Ig will be the last of their tribe.

One would think, after so many years, there would be a cure for the monster killing her mother. Yes, one would think with all the advances in medicine, even before the climate shifts, a cure for cancers and diseases such as this would be available.

But, no. All the medicine out there, it only staves the diseases and cancers off for just so long before the person finally can't take anymore and gives up.

Mom, Ig knows, will never stop fighting. It's in their blood, their heritage, to keep fighting.

Ig's gaze drifts from the floor to her mother, who lies on her side on the bed. Ig spots the mess, then quickly looks away. When she looks again, she takes in the frail thing her once strong mother has become. Her mother's hands are thin and curled at the second knuckle. It's as though all the muscle and life of them have been secretly drained away. She can't grip anything. Can't lift anything. All she can move are her thumbs. She needs better care than this, Ig knows. And with what Berk gave her tonight, maybe it's possible.

The woman on the bed is so thin, so fragile. But her spirit remains strong. And, to Ig, that's all that matters right now.

She helps Mom out of bed, gives her a bath and change of nightgowns. She strips the bed and throws away the sheets. The last of the bedding she owns goes onto Mom's bed.

Helping Mom to a chair at the dining room table, Ig asks, "I'll get you something to eat."

"Thank you. I love you."

Ig, once more, fights back tears. She straightens a bit, smiling as best as she can. "I love you too, Mom."

Before the waterworks come, she hurries to the kitchen and makes their supper. Oatmeal is the only thing they've been able to afford. Well, until Berkley gave her about one hundred thousand dollars. That, though, Ig has plans for. If she can use it to get Mom better help…

She places a bowl of oatmeal and cup of well water in front of her mother and watches as the woman fumbles with the spoon a bit before finally managing to scoop up some of the stuff and eat.

Ig was about to eat too, when Mom manages, "Why'd you get fired?"

"I didn't. Berk is throwing in the towel. He is almost ninety. Anyway, he's leaving and gave me my severance pay."

To this, Mom blinks. "He paid you?"

Ig nods. "Yep. Surprised me too."

"H—How much?"

Here is the tricky question she's been waiting for.

"Um, about fifty thousand."

Mom's face lights up and Ig's heart sinks. She hates lying to her mother. Always has, when she felt needed to do so.

This time, it's more about the surprise. If she can get real meds that work and actually heal Mom, the lie will be worth it. She refuses to think about the opposite. Surely, one hundred thousand will pay for something, right?

"That's great," Mom says, smiling as best she can. "We can get electricity back and real plumbing."

Ig nods, smiling and hating herself for it.

"We can fix this place up and have *real* food!"

Again, Ig nods and smiles. If it makes Mom feel better, then good.

She places a hand on Mom's withered one. "I love you, Mom."

The woman smiles. "Why, I love you too, sweetie. Are you alright?"

"I'm fine." Ig eats her oatmeal and wishes for eggs. She hasn't had eggs for over two years and just the thought of them sends pangs of nostalgia through her.

Mom lets it drop and finishes her oatmeal.

Once supper is finished, Ig places the bowls in the sink and plops down in the chair at the table again, exhausted, but…

She holds up a deck of old playing cards. "Rummy?" It's either rummy or poker with Mother. Despite the redundancy, Ig enjoys these evenings.

The woman smiles. "Always, my sweet girl."

Somewhere in the middle of the game, Mom says, "Your dad always loved rummy."

This pauses Ig. It's rare when Mom talks about Dad, even rarer if it's something specific. This is the first time Ig finds out her birth father played rummy. After all these years of playing the card game with Mom, finally it comes out.

Ig isn't really sure how to respond. She nods, then she frowns, then stares at her cards.

One of Mom's thin hands falls on Ig's wrist. Ig looks up. The woman's face softens, eyes glimmering in the candlelight. "He loved you, Ignia. The sea took him too soon."

She'd heard a lot of stories of her father over the years. All of them edging toward bad to nearly godlike. Depending on Mom's mood. There are many rumors of what happened. But the most famous one, and one both Mom and she believe the most (or at least wish to), is: Marcus Hawkins died out at sea when his crab boat sank. It's all either of them could manage to accept or hold on to.

Her father went missing when she was thirteen. No one ever found his body, nor the rest of the crew aboard The Breach.

Once Mom began losing the strength in her hands, Ig made her a card holder. Ig places her mother's cards in this now, lining them up carefully.

They play rummy into the night. Laughing and just enjoying each other's company.

Soon enough, it'll be Ig here in this old, small house with only the ghosts of the past to keep her company.

***

The next day brings with it two things: Mom's dry voice, and the knocking at the door.

Ig blinks, sitting up in bed. She glances at the window of her room. The sky melds from orange to bright pinks and pastel purples. Dawn edging toward morning.

Who would be knocking at their door so early?

She gets dressed, checks in on Mom quick.

"I'm fine, sweetie. But someone's at the door, I think."

"It woke you up too?"

She manages a frail nod

Ig growls deep in her throat and storms to the door. She unlocks it and swings it open.

"Who the hell—?"

"Ms. Hawkins?"

An older man with a graying beard and gleaming bald head stands on the stoop. He isn't exactly tall but average enough height. His blue eyes hold her gaze. There's something in those eyes which eases her a bit. A calm kindness she rarely encounters these days.

"Ig? Who is it?"

She glances away a moment. "I don't know yet, Mom. Hold on."

"Okay. Sorry."

Mom had been the strongest woman Ig knew before ALS sank its grotesque teeth in. For so many years, she fought and thrived. She endured.

And now…

"My name is Bracken Tull. Berkley asked me to stop by."

Why does that name sound so familiar? But where has she heard that name before? Something happened a few years ago and his name was mentioned. Nothing big. A small article in the paper, maybe?

He clears his throat. "I assume you're Ignia Hawkins?"

She nods, then shakes her head. "Yeah. Sorry. Come in."

He gives her a warm smile and steps inside. She shuts the door behind him and frowns.

"Do I know you from somewhere?"

Bracken grunts. "I doubt it. But maybe you heard my name a couple times."

Ig glances around. "Um, would you like to sit down? I can get some water. Fresh well water, if you like that?"

"Oh, I think I'm okay. No need to trouble yourself. Just wanted to stop by and see for myself the famous Ig Hawkins."

She snorts. "Famous? Oh, yeah, see…you're full of shit there, dude."

"Not at all. Your name pops up often within certain circles. When Berkley told me of his plans to retire and you might need work, I jumped at the chance to meet with you. Hope it's not too early?"

"Definitely too early, but, it's okay. What kind of jobs do you offer?"

Bracken smiles. "A very specific one. But I can't discuss it here. Could you meet me at Quint's Warf at around noon? I'll tell you everything you need to know there."

"Why not here?"

"Because, there will be more people involved than just you and me. Instead of repeating myself, I'd rather get it all done at once."

She nods. "Makes sense, I guess."

There's a moment of silence that's shattered by Mom.

"Ig? Who's here? I need help."

Ig lowers her head and looks up when he speaks.

"I understand your mother suffers from a disease?" Bracken's dark blue eyes hold her gaze.

"Y-yeah. ALS. There's no cure."

The softest smile brightens his otherwise haggard face. "There is, actually. You just need enough money to pay for it."

"How do you know?"

"I just know. We'll leave it at that for now." He walks toward the door, stops, and faces her. "I'll send someone here to take care of your mother while we're gone. A professional caregiver, so no need to worry."

A frown creases her face. "When are we leaving?"

He opens the door, looks back. "Right after our meeting at Quint's Warf. Noon. I hope to see you there."

And with this, he steps outside and closes the door behind him.

Ig stares at the door for a long time until Mom's urgent, worried voice breaks her out of the reverie.

"I need to go to the bathroom."

Wincing, Ig hurries to her mother's room and helps the dear woman to the bathroom. Then she ushers Mom to the dining room table, seating her.

"I haven't gone to the market yet," Ig says.

"Oh. Well, eggs do sound very good. Haven't had eggs for a long time."

"The market is two miles away. I need to be at Quint's Warf by noon. And that's about five miles away. On foot...that'll take me awhile."

Mom visibly withers. "Okay. Oatmeal, then."

Ig goes to make a couple bowls when Mom says, "Who was in our house, Ig?"

She stops and turns back to her mother. "A man who's going to give me work. He'll be sending someone here to take care of you while I'm gone."

Mom's gaze drifts away. "Can we trust this man?"

"I think so. Yes. But, I really don't see any other choice right now. I need to make money. And he says there's a cure."

To this, Mom straightens a bit. "There isn't a cure, Ig. You know that. He can't be—"

"I'll go the meeting at noon and see what else he says. If I find something off, I'll come back home. Deal?"

She manages a weak nod. "Deal."

"I have to do something, Mom. And if there's a cure...we can stop all this and be happy again."

Mom's face softens. "Oh, my sweet girl, I *am* happy. This disease isn't the end of me, and I'm so very proud of you."

"I love you too, but don't you want to be able to be yourself again?"

Her mother nods. "Well, yes. But this is what the Great Spirits want. It's not right to meddle in their ways, you know. I have made my peace with it."

"Mom, I refuse to believe the Great Spirits would want you to be suffering like this."

"They have their own reasons," Mom says. "And so, we must abide by those reasons."

There's nothing Ig can say to this. It's the way of their tribe. The way of many tribes, in a way. Dying means returning to the Earth from which life is born.

"I'm still going to see what he has to say," Ig says, feeling her mother's disapproval at her back as she enters the small kitchen.

She builds a fire in the stove and goes about cooking their oatmeal for breakfast.

It's not long after they finish eating, when another knock on the door blasts through the silence of the house.

Floorboards creak under her as Ig hurries to the door and opens it.

A woman, maybe somewhere in her forties, smiles. "Hello. Is this the Hawkins residence?" Her salt and pepper hair was buzzed short.

"Yeah," Ig says. "Who are you?"

The woman nods and holds out a hand. "Vivian Wendt. RN. Bracken Tull sent me to take care of your mother while you're away."

Ig shakes her hand. "Okay. Come on in. But I'm not sure you'll be staying long."

The older woman blinks. "Is that so?"

"Well, I haven't exactly accepted whatever Bracken is offering yet."

Vivian smiles. "Of course. May I meet your mother?"

Ig nods. "Sure. She's in the dining room." She leads the woman to mother and steps aside, carefully observing. This is the person who will be taking care of Mom while she's gone, after all. Any red flags and the bitch is gone.

Vivian sat right down next to Mom. "Hello, hun. I'm Vivian Wendt. I'm a registered nurse sent to care for you while your daughter is away."

Mom looks from Vivian to Ig, then back again. "Where's Ig going?"

Ig opens her mouth to tell her, but Vivian beats her to it.

"A meeting. And if the meeting proves well, she'll be gone a couple weeks. If the mission is successful, we have found a cure for ALS."

It takes a moment, but Mom finally says, "This is a real cure?"

Vivian smiles and Ig feels it's genuine. "Yes. I wouldn't be here if I felt it wasn't. I'm a stickler for facts."

Mom stares at the woman for a long time before finally saying, "Okay. Just never really trust white people before."

Again, Vivian smiles. And, unless the woman is an extremely good actor, Ig sees and feels nothing but truth. Watching all this, Ig doesn't exactly trust the woman without a doubt, but enough…just enough, perhaps, to ease her nerves.

Then they begin to talk. For over an hour, Ig notes before getting herself ready to meet Bracken.

Neither of them seem to notice when she slips out the door.

CHAPTER 3

Quint's Warf is nothing more than ancient, metal pylons. So rusted, they're merely spikes stabbing out of the water.

A skeleton of what it used to be. Which, according to many stories, was the first in overseas trade. A long-ago business that never really panned out.

The business dried up and soon the company owning Quint's Warf moved away, leaving their investment to rot over time.

And rot it did…

Now, as Ig gathers with a small crowd, she can't help but wonder why Bracken chose to meet here in the first place. It's not protected from the elements, nor boasts integrity.

Still, the man himself stands before a group of, perhaps, fifty men and women.

A chilly wind whips off the Pacific Ocean, sending a series of shivers through Ig. With her boots buried in the sand, she curses Bracken for taking so damn long.

He stands on a slightly elevated platform.

The others mingle, chatting away, while Ig stands on the outside watching. There doesn't appear to be fifty people, as Bracken said, but probably around twenty. They all seem to know each other too. Or at least heard of one another. Seagulls cry, circling the wharf. Vultures of the sea, some call them.

It's okay, though, she's used to being the outsider. Likes it this way. She can observe, get a feel for the people around her. Their social behaviors, or perhaps even slivers of their personality.

Her mind drifts to Mom, however. Is Vivian taking good care of her? Can she really trust these people? She's about to give up and head back home when a rusty jeep barrels down a slight embankment and skids to a stop.

Bracken and some other man get out and trudge through the sand toward the group. Everyone has fallen silent as the two men approach. The man opposite of Bracken is of slighter build. Has almost a nerdy look to him. All except for his eyes, which are dark and focused. His face is gaunt, dark hair a mess on his head. Both men are wearing black tactical gear.

"Okay," Bracken shouts over the waves. "Thank you all for trusting me and coming here. Some of you know who I am, but the rest of you, I assume, don't. I'm Bracken Tull, the sole survivor of the Leviathan attack that claimed the lives of my entire team. I have promises to keep that I've waited too long to act on." His gaze drifts over the people, rests on Ig. She squirms a bit, though not entirely uncomfortable under this gaze. "And, although I have taken care of something, there's still unfinished business to be had."

No one speaks. No one moves. All their attention is on Bracken.

"Miles?" Bracken gestures at the black man in the group. "Would you like to tell us a bit about your experience quick?"

Miles joins Bracken and the other man. He gives a nod to the group.

Ig frowns, knowing she's seen his face before, though not sure where.

"Well," Miles says, "I'm not really sure where to begin." He shrugs. "For the sake of this operation, I'll skim it. A couple years ago, I was asked to assist in a mission to stop a creature that had no right existing. Jörmungandr. Yeah, the ancient Norse sea serpent." He sighs. "Sounds crazy, but the evidence is in Government custody now. Well, as far as I know. I accepted only because it attacked the battleship my brother was on. I didn't care about that thing. I wanted to find my brother. But, my old Seal team, the Dagger Points, intercepted. Apparently, they saved me from the asshole who was trying to employ me. Anyway, I set out with them to find my brother, but what we found was madness. It…it got into my head." Miles steps away, back facing the group, head lowered.

Ig moves in closer to the group. She's heard something like this story before. From the news, or something. But…

"I killed my team. It…it got in my head and I killed them all except for two. It altered reality, or something just as fucked up." He faces the group, tears trickling down his cheeks. "Only way to kill it was with one of Fenrir's fangs. In Norse mythology, that's like its sibling, I guess. Anyway, long story short, I sent a laser burst with that fang fixed in the cap directly into the bastard's eye."

Everyone stares at him. Like with Bracken, no one moves.

Finally, Bracken places a hand on Mile's shoulder. "Thank you. I know it's hard. Believe me."

Miles shrugs away from him. "You…you don't know, man. Until you've personally murdered your friends, your family, you don't know."

"You're right. I don't. But it wasn't your fault. You know that, right?"

Nodding, Miles wipes away tears. "Yeah. Anyway, I got the weapons you wanted."

Bracken pats Mile's shoulder. "You rock."

But Miles doesn't respond. He steps back in with the group, silent, brow low and brooding.

Bracken visibly sighs and takes center stage again. "With all of us, there's one underlying theme. One bastard who connects us all. The villain, I guess you'd say." He gives the group a glance. "Murdock Jones."

A murmur passes through the crowd.

Ig blinks.

Murdock Jones? The oil guy?

She can see him being the villain, though. His company, MJ Oil, has stolen much of her tribe's land and planted small oil rigs everywhere. This alone marks him as an asshole in her book. But how does he connect everyone, as Bracken says? Did he employ them all at one point? Betray them...? Probably both, knowing what little she knew of the man. Which is all not good.

Bracken says, "He's had his fingers in everything related to rare sea creatures and," he shoots a glance at the other man, "lake monsters." Bracken looks at the group, though Ig feels like his gaze never strays too far from her. "I've been monitoring him throughout the years. Tapped into his communications with help from Leigh here." He points at a woman standing near the front of the group. "Most recently, we intercepted communication, which leads me to now. All of you are supposed to be employed by MJ Oil right now."

Someone in the group, not far from Ig, says, "The hell? I could use the money. I don't care if he's an asshole. I have six kids to feed."

With a firm nod, Bracken says, "And you would've been paid very well, Mrs. Collins. Although, as he works, you would never live to see all that money he promises. In fact, like me, he might even pit everything against you, so you won't make it out alive."

Mrs. Collins shakes her head, though says no more.

"Do you all want to know what your collective mission was going to be?"

Another murmur rolls through the group.

"He wanted to send all of you out on a cruiser to capture a mermaid."

"Well," someone in the groups spouts. "They're real, so I imagine he wants to learn from them, or see if they can cure cancers in some way?"

Bracken shakes his head. "Yes, mermaids are real, but the reason why he wanted one alive is a bit...messed up."

Ig watches, fascinated despite herself.

"He has no moral gain, just to be the first to catch a live mermaid and sell it to an aquarium or highest bidder. If he couldn't sell it, he planned to cut it up and toss it back into the ocean. This is the man we're dealing with here. A man who deceives and just doesn't plain care about anyone but himself."

There's a beat of silence, then...

"So, what do you want from us?" a woman to the far right asks. "I have better things to do than stand here and listen to shit I already know."

"Fair enough," Bracken says. "I stole you from him for a purpose. One that will end all this insanity and set things to right." He smiles a bit. "I want you to help me kill the Mother of Monsters."

Everyone pauses. Ig frowns. For a few long, seconds, the only sounds are the waves crashing against the pylons of the old wharf.

"Okay," Miles says, moving just a bit in front of the group. "What the hell is, 'The Mother of Monsters'?"

A roll of thunder pauses Bracken's words before he can speak them. So quickly the weather changes nowadays. Only moments ago, it was spring! Now, middle November.

"And how do you know this 'mother' exists?" someone else asks.

Bracken smiles the tiniest bit. Barely visible through his beard. "Because, if any of you survived the mermaid capture, you were to be sent to take samples from the thing. From what we've gathered over the past few weeks, this is the one. She has the ability to birth both extinct species, and fairly mythological. Or, like the Leviathan...hybrids."

"Hold on," Miles says, once more stepping away from the group. "You telling me this 'mother' is responsible for all the crazy shit going on out there?"

Bracken shrugs. "Maybe. Most of it, I'm willing to bet."

Miles frowns at Bracken. "I do believe you're talking out your ass."

"I wish I was. But I've checked and double checked. She's out there, giving birth to monsters."

"But how do you *know*?"

Sighing, Bracken says, "Among other things, I also intercepted information about a large, organic mass in the Devil's Trench. Deepest section of the Pacific. With more research and having a few folks check and recheck...yeah, that has to be her. Every seven days, smaller masses float away from the original mass. Which, I believe, is her offspring."

There's a chink in Bracken's reasoning, though...

"That mass could be anything," Ig says. "Do you have absolute proof it's this 'mother'?"

He frowns at her. "No. Nothing absolute or definitive."

"Say this thing is real," Miles says. "What do we get if we help you kill it? Not trying to sound greedy, but this is a serious mission you want us to go on. People could die. And, I'm sure you understand, I have enough blood on my hands."

The man standing next to Bracken steps forward. His bookish face is firm, gaze surveying the small crowd. "My experience isn't like Bracken's or Miles's, but I lost my own people in Lake Superior a couple years ago. The operation was set up and orchestrated by Murdock Jones. We accidentally unthawed a *Dunkleosteus*. Mr. Jones wanted to capture and test it. We wanted to get it back to the ocean through underground tunnels. Both attempts failed, and it took its hunger out on us. Eighty people died down there." He looks away, as though thinking about what next to say.

"Sorry for your losses, man," Miles says. "But what does any of that have to do with this proposed mission?"

"Because I found the real location of it. Also, I can pinpoint it and show a visual."

"You serious?"

The man nods and holds up a paper-thin tablet. He taps a few things, then turns it around to show Miles. "This is the Mother of Monsters."

Ig is too far away to see clearly, but Miles eventually lowers his head.

"This picture was taken by a satellite over the region ten minutes ago," the man with the tablet says. "She's real. And I believe she's responsible for the unusual influx of monsters out there."

"I see she's real," Miles says. "But that doesn't change the fact of any of this being worthwhile. No pay. What, are we just supposed to accept this and go out there for the pure glory of it?"

"Yes," Bracken boomed. "That's exactly what we do. We go out there. We kill her. We end the creation of more monsters. The seas will stabilize after some time. As it is, the fish are scarce because of all the behemoths out there. Even sharks are rare." He pats the younger man on the shoulder. "Thanks, Ash." Then his stern gaze drifts over everyone. "This is it. This is how we save the oceans. This is how we spit in Murdock's face. This is how finally win."

Miles nods. "Oh, I'm with you. But it's hard enough to make a living this day and age, not all of us can afford to take a week off to go monster hunting. You see what I mean?"

"Yup," Bracken says. "That's why Murdock is going to pay you."

Everyone, Ig included, appears to blink. All their attention is on Bracken, with his bald head, graying beard, and intense gaze.

He smiles, kindly enough. "That, you all need to trust me on."

"So," a woman in the group shouts over the crashing waves. "We're supposed to trust someone like you, who let his crew die?" She grunts. "Yeah, let me get right on that." She turns, pushes her way through the group, and walks away.

Ig frowns after the woman, coughs, and absently takes a puff of her inhaler. For a moment, she almost follows the lady.

"Look," Bracken says. "I'm not keeping anyone here against their will. You need to want to do this. I can't make solid promises, but you can trust me to be honest."

A few others shake their head and slip away from the group.

By the time all is said and done, they're down to about a dozen people, not including Bracken, Ash, and Ig.

Miles steps to the front of the smaller group, places a hand on Bracken's shoulder. "Do I want to get paid for the work I do? Hell yeah I do. But…you know the more I think about it, the more I understand what Bracken is trying to say. This is more than money. This is a chance to right the oceans. If life in the oceans die, we'll soon follow."

"I doubt that," a man right beside Ig said.

Miles blinked. "Doubt what, exactly?"

"Well, shit, we don't even know if this mother monster exists. You can point out satellite images all day, but I'm still not fully convinced. Those images are too grainy to really tell what that mass is. And let's say it does exist. You really think it's producing so many sea monsters daily that they'll chomp down all the sea life?"

"You sound like all those climate change naysayers before Earth proved them wrong decades ago."

"More like a climate shift," Ash mutters.

Miles waves a dismissive hand. "Okay. Whatever. The point is, just because you don't have all the evidence, doesn't mean it's not happening."

The man standing beside Ig puffs his cheeks out in a breath. Just above a whisper, he says, "This is nuts." But he didn't move, and Ig respects him for it.

She agrees with him, though. This is nuts. Suicidal, even. Who in their right mind, without any military aid, would head out to the deepest point of the Pacific Ocean to kill a "Mother of Monsters" no one is for sure exists, while everyone knows big creatures stalk those waters? Doesn't sit very well with her.

On the other hand, she's curious. What did Bracken say about money? That Murdock Jones is going to pay everyone? How, if Bracken intercepted all of Murdock's leads? And what if the old tycoon figures out what's happening? This latter drives a thin, cold spike in her stomach. She's heard plenty of stories about the man to know he will just as soon kill you than deal with any negative aspects.

"Took me a sec to realize just who ya are," an older man in a faded, red baseball cap says, shuffling out of the crowd toward Bracken. "You're the dumbass who invented those diggin' mechs but, somehow went broke. How the hell does an inventor and designer of special mechs go broke, hmm?"

Bracken withers a bit. "I used the mechs to further my business, and when everything began to dry up, I sold the designs to someone, and they ended up not paying me. I couldn't afford to drill for water. But, can you guess who 'bought' my designs?"

The older man nods. "Yup. Was Murdock Jones. Damn tragedy. But, didn't ya have a good friend? What's his name…Seth?"

To this, Bracken straightens. His brow furrows and Ig can practically feel the tension in the air tightening and tightening like hundreds of thin cables. She steps away from the group. Not far but being too close felt wrong right then.

The older man holds up a liver-spotted hand. "Easy, son. Not tryin' to get yer goat, here. I'm with ya. Just tryin' to understand your reasoning b'hind everything at that time."

It took a moment, but Bracken finally said, "Pride. Pride and stupidity. If I had listened to Seth, no one would've died." He glances away, face contorting into something between anger and sorrow. "I live with this every day. Keeps me up nights. Those ghosts. Everything during that time, I was on the verge of insanity, I think. And Murdock Jones capitalized on my weakness."

The older man nodded. "Fair enough. We're all human, after all. Flawed. We let our emotions, or lack of, get the best of us, am I right?"

"Yeah," Bracken says. "I've had a lot of time to get myself back on track. Been tapping into Mr. Jones's communications. This is how we end him. He stays rich with these monsters."

"How?" Ig spouts without thinking.

Bracken's gaze falls on her. "He profits from selling them to the highest bidders. Trophy enthusiasts. Self-proclaimed scientists. And, of course, the Government. He produces and sells oil, but it's the little side businesses that keep him wealthy."

Ig nods. It makes sense. The only problem she has is…

"Why did you accept going to the Ghost Rig Sera, anyway? And how do we know you're not making some off-the-cuff decision like you did back then?"

He shrugs. "I wasn't exactly in my right mind at the time, like I said. I've studied Murdock's comms for a few years now. Watching and listening. If not for him, a lot of people would still be alive, and I'm not just talking about my beloved crew. Miles, Ash, they know too."

Ash nods. Miles lowers his head.

Ig gives Bracken, Ash, and Miles a final nod, and falls silent. She has no argument, and nothing rebuts Bracken's reasoning for what happened...what? Five years ago, now? Long enough to let it go, in any case.

Bracken was a case of controversy, if she remembers right. Many believed he made it all up to get some publicity to get his business back on track. Others claimed some huge Government conspiracy, which hid a lot of information from the public, making Bracken appear worse than what he was.

And what was he?

Ig doesn't have to dwell on it long.

Bracken is a lost man. He's a haunted man. Probably more lost during the time of Murdock Jones than now. During the time of the Leviathan. A story that was little more than a paragraph in the news, which pretty much labeled Bracken crazy.

But Ig can tell he's still lost. His experience has taken something away from him. An inner shine, perhaps? Something which kisses the eyes alight and a smile fixed to widen. Whatever truly brought happiness to Bracken is just as unknown as what lurks beneath the sea. To look at Bracken is to look upon a haunted man.

He runs a hand over his beard, gaze on Ig. He sighs. "You remind me of my daughter." Tears glisten in his eyes. He spins away before they spill down his cheeks. Back to the dwindling group, he says, "She died shortly after we reconnected."

"I'm sorry," Ig says, heart aching for him.

"Don't be. She got some sand in a cut back home. The infection spread so fast she never had a chance. The doctors tried, but..." He trails off, shaking his head.

The older man lowers his head. "Well, maybe we better get this done, eh? In your daughter's honor."

Bracken nods and faces the group again. "Yes. Let's get it done." He wipes a stray tear from his cheek. "Time to end it."

CHAPTER 4

Ig follows the others to a black bus idling near the beach. She gives the ocean a glance, shivers scuttling through her. There are things out there. Massive, hungry things. And as their food supply dwindles, the more dangerous they'll become.

But, is ending them completely really answer?

Her throat tightens a bit and she uses her inhaler. A few seconds later, everything eases. Her throat, lungs, and nerves. Well—

"You think you can be in a mech for hours?"

Ig nearly screams, whirls around to find Bracken smiling gently at her. His haunted eyes held her gaze. "I, uh, I don't know. Never been in one."

He taps the inhaler still clutched in her hand. "You won't be able to use that in a mech."

This plunges an icy spike into her stomach. "Well, I...I think I'll be okay." A lie. Anything too stressful or if she overexerts herself, she needs the inhaler. Thank the shitty air quality these days, or the poor, cockroach-infested environment she was born in. Blame some flaw in her gene pool. Blame everything, but it won't change the fact she's limited in many ways.

When cures were actually being sought after, perhaps asthma should've been toward the top along with ALS and AIDS. If they can find a cure for Parkinson's disease, they should be able to figure out the others, right?

It's an argument she waged with herself for years, even more so since Mom was diagnosed.

Bracken's gentle smile never falters. "There's no guarantee you'll get paid. If you want to bow out, there's no shame in it."

And, for a moment, she considers this. She'll just have to figure out another way to get money. Besides, she was a fool to think she'd be able to go out and fight sea monsters like a badass she is not. She might be the best at illegally collecting things for buyers, but as far as being a warrior...not so much.

Yet...

"I'll stay."

His smile fades some. "Are you absolutely sure? I'm serious. If you feel you can't do this, there's no shame in bowing out."

She straightens, getting a little pissed off now. "I said I'll be okay."

Bracken grunts. "Somehow, I knew that'd be your answer."

"So, Berk didn't really call you?"

"No. He called an advocate for Murdock Jones, which was routed to the man himself. You were to be put on a crew to help collect mermaids off a rocky island in the South Pacific called Manutu. Soon as I gathered this information, I called and met with the others, along with yourself. Murdock's men will be arriving tomorrow to gather you and the others for the mission."

Ig frowns. "You said something about Murdock paying us?"

"Yes. A transaction of one hundred million dollars was made shortly after the mission was declared. I intercepted it and had my team route the money to a separate bank account. If all works out, you and everyone here should get at least five million. Probably more."

Well, this is something she can work with, for sure. It's no guarantee, but, so far, it's the best she can hope for.

"One million," Bracken says, "and we might be able to cure your mother. Might. Depends how advanced she is in the disease."

Ig's heart sinks. "She's pretty bad."

Bracken nods, strokes his beard. "So, you have a choice to make. I won't tell you which way the right way is, because there is no right way. I'm getting on the bus. If you choose to go home, great. No harm done, and no one will think less of you. In fact, if all goes well, I'll pay for your mother's treatments. You don't even have to go."

He places a hand on her shoulders, smiles, and tromps up the steps into the bus.

Ig stares after him, gaze lifting to the driver, who appears less than impressed with her. Indeed, he appears bored and on the verge of passing out. Those dark crescents under his eyes are tell-tale signs of too many nights where sleep eluded him.

She turns back to the ocean. The afternoon sun glistens off its moving surface. By all accounts, something so beautiful shouldn't harbor such terrors. And yet…it does. The sea will always hold mysteries and dangers. Vastly still unexplored, the sea will always thrive. Life always finds a way to go on.

"Well," a craggy voice spouts behind her. "Ya comin' or goin'?"

Ig puffs air through her lips. "Coming." She turns and steps onto the bus.

Sometimes, risks need to be taken.

Besides, Mom is being taken care of.

***

All the windows on the bus are painted black and each seat is enclosed because, secrets, apparently.

It isn't long before Bracken says, "It's best you don't know the location of where we're going, so just sit tight everyone. We'll be there in about a half hour."

"Anyone else feel like they've been had?" someone says.

No one answers and the bus trundles onward to whatever destination it's set for.

Ig leans back, a sigh whispering through her lips. Taped to the back of the seat ahead of her is a worn sheet of paper. A brown smear graces the upper right corner. She blinks and leans forward again. A frown creases her brow as she reads:

We are those who stand up. We are those who fight. Against evil and tyranny. Against years of corruption. We are the Resistance. YOU are the Resistance. Time to FIGHT!

She leans back once more, heart thudding heavily. *What the hell is this?*

The question doesn't go unanswered for long.

"What's this shit mean?" a voice which sounds like the older man asks. Probably it is.

"I assume you mean the paper," Bracken says. "You'll see what that means soon."

"What the hell did you just trick us into, Bracken?" This is Miles, as far as Ig can tell.

"Nothing. Just wait and see."

Chatter rises among the people on the bus, even though no one can see each other. As for Ig, she sits quietly, reading the paper and its message over and over.

She's heard of the Resistance before. A lot, though, never any real evidence of such. No groups. No protests for the last decade or so.

It was said the so-called Resistance had accepted defeat and disbanded.

Unless the papers on the back of the seats are old, they mean the Resistance is still very much alive. She's always believed in those people even if she couldn't afford to join them emotionally. She'd have to leave Mom. And this she couldn't do, even five years ago. When your family is reduced to two, it's more valuable to the spirit to stay and share with the remaining family member.

For Ig's tribe, the little known Syvwa, family is all that's left. Once Mom is gone, only Ig will remain. Well, unless this mission kills her. Which is very possible.

And if this is really a Resistance bus…? Yeah, there's no guarantee on anything now.

The door to her seat opens and Ash pokes his head in. His dark hair spills onto a pasty forehead. "No one is letting me sit with them. Okay if I join you?"

Ig's first reaction is to tell him no. Instead, she nods. "Yes." She scoots over to the window side of the bench seat.

"Hey, thanks." Ash slips in and shuts the flimsy door. "I'm Ash, by the way." He extends a hand.

Ig chuckles. "I know." But, as she's shaking his hand and just about to release, she pauses. Her gaze fixes on a wad of gauze wrapped around his wrist.

He notices her gaze and slips his hand back quickly. "Not what you think."

She snaps a frown at him. "Then what happened?"

Ash doesn't look at her. "Long story."

Smiling, Ig places a hand on his arm. "We have time, I think."

He looks at her, eyes shiny with either tears, or hope. She isn't sure. Regardless, she keeps her smile and nods.

A ragged breath fights its way out him. He turns to her a bit more. "I'm not going to tell you my entire story, but I was part of a team in Lake Superior. I was told there were unusual fossils there. Well, we accidentally unthawed a *Dunkleosteus*. Big placoderm fish of the Devonian Period. Sometimes nicknamed The Guillotine. Anyway, it woke up and killed a lot of people, including a few I held dear. I barely made it."

She's heard of this story before. Once again, it was nothing more than a vague article in the news. Nothing to garner much attention. Even though, like Bracken's, it should've been huge, front page news. Come to think of it, she remembers reading something about Miles too, and the Norse serpent. All three appear to have been covered up, or at least watered down, their stories twisted. No doubt Murdock Jones was behind it all. Funny how the man slithers through lives like a venomous snake, poisoning everyone in his wake.

"Anyway," Ash continues, gaze drifting away from her. "I woke up in a white room, bound to a bed. Like in a hospital. He was there too." He looks away, visibly shuddering.

"What happened?"

It takes him a few minutes to respond. "There were razor blades in the restraints around my wrists." Once again, he shivers. "Every move I made, the deeper the blades cut. He left me like that. My punishment for not—wait, why am I even telling you all this?"

Ig smiles, pats his arm. "Because, maybe, you need someone to listen?" Hard to tell if this is the case, but it feels right. He needs to tell someone, even if others already know. He needs this release. And, maybe he's told the very same story a few times already. She doesn't know, but the more he talks about it, the better he'll be. The more he can face the anger and fear—and gods knows he's probably had his fair share—the more he can destroy it.

For, fear cannot thrive if it is crushed under a boot heel.

Ash favors Ig with a weak smile. "Thanks."

"Sure," she says, returning the smile.

He fetches a sigh. "So, yeah. Murdock left me to die alone in that room. And I thought I was going to. I don't know how long it took, but the next thing I knew, Bracken and a couple other guys broke down the door. Got me medical attention." His gaze lowers a bit. "Guess I lost a lot of blood and if Bracken had been fifteen minutes late, I would've been dead."

Ig keeps her smile. "So, Bracken saved you. That's why you're here."

He shrugs. "Mostly. But he can also use my expertise in Prehistoric Anthropology."

Ig's smile morphs into a frown. "Is that even a thing?"

Ash snorts. "Never used to be. When the climate shifts happened and after Civil War II, the Government was suddenly interested in how dinosaurs died and how they might have lived. So, basically, they mixed archeology and anthropology into its own beast."

She was only about seven years old when the second Civil War broke out over America. A fast and brutal war, which laid waste to nearly everything, but she remembers how scared her mother was. The worry and the preparation, just in case the Reds made it far enough west. So many people, from New York to Texas, died in that meaningless war. A war which introduced genetically engineered creatures to America. Things so vicious, it took another two years to subdue populations once the war was over. Fortunately, the Reds didn't quite make it far enough west before a truce was announced.

Ig, intrigued, shifts, so she faced him fully. "And how did you become a Prehistoric Anthropologist? You're pretty young, right?"

"I'm thirty-six." He shrugs. "Guess that's pretty young, but I started out in anthropology."

"What made you want to figure out how dinosaurs died?"

"It's really not like that. We all know how they all died, but some...they died by other means. And that's what I was often hired to do. Or, at the very least, identify what species was found in some remote island."

She nods. "Nice. Pay well?"

"Yeah. Not too bad. Made most of my money through subcontracting, though. Being Government official paid little to nothing in the grand scheme of things. What's your name, by the way?"

"Ig," she says, not giving him her full name. If there's one thing she's learned in life, it's to never trust anyone. No matter how kind they appear.

The bus stops with a jolt and squeal.

A moment later, Bracken announces, "We're here. Meet me outside."

Ash sighs, gives Ig a final smile, and exits the closed-in seat. People mutter to one another as they shuffle through the aisle.

Ig waits a moment, then follows the others out of the bus.

CHAPTER 5

"There is no name for the place you're about to enter," Bracken shouts over the wind. "Anyone who asks where we are will be transported away."

A man so white he might as well be albino, says, "The fuck is this? You didn't say anything about some secret place, or the Resistance."

Bracken sighs, lowers his head, and points at the man.

Two very big men round the bus and grip Mr. Albino by the arms. He struggles.

"What the hell? I agreed to help!"

Bracken narrows his gaze on the man. "I can't have muddled thought here."

"You mean actual logic. Tell these oafs to let me go. I want to help!"

"I'm sure you do," Bracken says, "but I think it's for the wrong reasons. Take care of your family, Roger. I hear hunting cyos is pretty lucrative these days."

Roger doesn't get a chance to respond. One of the big men shoot him in the neck with something and he falls limp in their arms. They drag him away. Ig never sees him again.

"Sorry about that. As I was saying, no questions about the location. Once inside, you follow *all* the rules. Every single one. If not, you'll be transported out. This is a secured place. Any hint of Red rhetoric, you're gone. Understood?"

A gradual, "Yes," shivers through the group.

Ig merely nods. She gets it. Though, she realizes, this mission is becoming more about politics than the actual cause. Not what she wants to get into. All her life she's tried to avoid politics. Mainly because she needed income to care for her and Mother. If her employers leaned Red, then so be it.

Money is money.

This, though. This is something else.

The Resistance? Feels more like a prison in some ways. So many rules.

Above, the sky is settling nicely into early afternoon with the hazy sun warming directly above. Seagulls screech. Every time the birds do, she notes, Bracken cringes a little. So, he has a slight distaste for seagulls. Which is reasonable since Ig hates them too.

Never could stand those savaging bastards.

She forces herself to ignore their cries when Bracken says, "I didn't pick any of you randomly. You each possess a specific skill set which can aid the mission. Of course, you can opt out, if you wish. No shame in it. But here's your official chance. If you don't feel you can go on with the mission, say so now. We are very Blue here."

No one says anything. Even so, Bracken waits a few more minutes. The winds slow to a tepid breeze. When everyone appears set, he says. "Okay. Good. Let's get this started. Follow me."

Bracken strides ahead of the group. Ash and Miles pace him. The group, now barely ten in all, including Ig, follow.

Really, is there any other choice?

She's not very impressed with the squat, gray building in front of them. Growing up, Ig always envisioned the Resistance to at least boast something of class, or strength.

Instead, there's only this gray, bleak thing no larger than a mediocre warehouse. The door is just an ordinary steel door. Nothing special. Noting like she imagined a place where the fabled Resistance holed up.

Sometimes imagination tricks a person. Sometimes it gets out of hand and we create fantasies to distort reality. Might be harmless enough, at first. But after years and years of letting imagination take hold, all there exists is fantasy.

Seeing such a tired, gray building, Ig's heart sinks some.

Surrounding the old building is a rusty, equally tired-looking chain-link fence, topped with lazy loops of razor wire.

Bracken leads them to the gates, which, for a wonder, appear a little less weary and actually stand up straight. He unlocks the padlock and pulls the chains free. The gates swing open and he ushers everyone through.

"Head for the door," says. "I'll lock up."

Silence drapes over the group as they make their way to the door of the building. Ig glances over her shoulder just as Bracken coils the chains through the inner gate posts and snaps the padlock shut.

Maneuvering through group, Miles favors Ig with a smile before calling out to Bracken. "Door's locked."

Bracken nods and hurries over. "I know." He pats Miles on the shoulder and they both work their way through the group to the door.

Ig can't see anything over others and curses her family genes for the billionth time for being so short.

A click and a loud squawking sound. She manages to see the top of the door swing open. Barely two seconds after, and the group is filing through. No more than a dozen, but damn, they're like giants compared to her. Move like giants too. So slow it's maddening. Absently, Ig sucks down a puff from her inhaler.

The moment she steps across the threshold, the door squawks again. She spins, backing up, and the door slams shut. Darkness, complete and cold, envelopes her. She stretches her arms out before her, feeling for a wall, anything to bring a little orientation. Her hands find nothing but the chilly air. A whine crawls up her throat, heart trip-hammering. Sweat beads on her forehead, despite the cold air.

A hand grips her arm.

She screams, thrashing and kicking at whatever clutches her arm. She punches at it with her free fist. Bracken led them all into a trap. There are things in this dark room and they want to rip the flesh from her bones. They want to—

"Whoa-whoa! Settle down." The hand holding her arm releases.

She doesn't recognize the voice, though the terror squeezing her eases. Her breathing is a chaotic mess and she fumbles for the inhaler in her jeans pocket; even if she really doesn't need the medicine, it's a comfort. The only thing constant in her life, besides Mom. It's not albuterol, like one gets at pharmacies. She can't afford insurance, let alone the grossly inflated prices of the medicine itself.

She had to learn how to make her own version of albuterol and pressurize it in a small canister. There were many trials and errors, but she eventually perfected it. Granted, her own version isn't quite as effective as albuterol, but it stops the attacks, nonetheless. She keeps ten canisters on her always.

Including now.

Light flickers a second or two before the entire room is so bright, she has to close her eyes for a moment. A low hum of electricity flows through the air.

"Sorry about that," Bracken says. "Lights were supposed to be on."

Ig slowly opens her eyes. Her vision clears, gaping at a woman no taller than herself. A woman maybe in her late thirties with bright red hair and a spray of freckles across the bridge of her narrow nose. She smiles, and Ig can't help but smile back. Some smiles are just so addictive. And attractive. Those lips…

Ig's heart thudded. Dove wings flutter from her stomach to her chest.

"Sorry," Ig manages, fully embarrassed for her overreaction in the dark.

"Psshh," the red-haired woman says, waving a hand. "Been attacked in the dark worse than that, hun." She cocks a pencil thin eyebrow. "What's your name?"

"I…" She clears her throat, trying to stow the fluttering of those proverbial dove wings inside her. "Ignia."

The woman smiles big. "Such a gorgeous name. I'm Verity."

"Hi, Verity," Ig says, lips numb. She's never felt this way before and it kind of scares her.

Verity giggles. "Hi, Ignia."

"Ig."

Verity nods. "Ig, it is." She winks. "But I really like Ignia."

Heat blossoms through Ig's face.

"Okay," Bracken says, severing the connection between Ig and Verity being made. "We have to take the elevator down. Only five at a time."

The group surges forward and Ig eventually loses Verity in the shuffle. She sighs and follows the others, soon finding herself standing next to Miles.

He favors her with yet another smile. "Pretty crazy, huh?"

She nods, not sure what to say.

She's heard about him from the news too. Like Bracken. Though his article was even less informative, and also painted him as sort of a bad guy. He did, after all, kill most of his crew. Even if he claimed it was because the massive, mythical, sea serpent got in his head, she's not entirely convinced yet. To be honest, she's not convinced about any of them. Maybe Ash, but Bracken…yeah, she's still not sure about him either.

Ahead, five people, including Bracken, step onto the elevator.

The doors close and Miles turns to her. He leans close to Ig's ear, hot breath tickling her lobe. "Bracken wants you to attend a meeting in the Romus Room."

When Ig frowns at him, Miles shakes his head and places a hand on her shoulder. "Private meeting. You won't be alone. Soon as you exit the elevator, turn left."

With that, he moves to the head of their group. Ig's the last one on the elevator.

They descend five floors before stopping.

As soon as the elevator doors open, Ig realizes why the outside appears so tired and abandoned. It's all a disguise. A way to hide from the Reds, the Government, and everyone else. Camouflage. The polished, stainless steel walls reflect the group once the doors are fully open and all Ig can do is stare at herself while the others pile out. There's a mirror at home, but she rarely ever looks into it. Too busy to make sure her hair is brushed and face washed. She's always despised makeup, so she never really needs a mirror.

Besides, Mom always said mirrors can be portals to other worlds. Other times. And, sometimes, things can slip through those mirrors into our world. Bad things. Things that bite.

Regardless, Ig sighs at her haggard mess of a reflection. Dark hair a nest of snarls. Face smeared here and there with dirt. She's long become accustom to her own odor, but what is it like for everyone else?

No one has complained, but, still.

"Ig?"

She shakes her head and finds Verity. The ghost of a smile plays at her pink lips. A thin eyebrow lifts. Arms cross over her chest.

"Uh, hey," Ig manages.

"So, um, everyone is that way. I guess we're supposed to go this way?" She points to the left of the elevator.

Ig snaps out of it and nods. "Oh! Yeah. This way, I think. Wait, you too?"

"Yep," Verity says. "Miles told me to meet Bracken in some place called the Romus Room."

"Well," Ig says. "Guess we better get there then?"

Verity snorts. "You okay? You sound weird. I mean, you sounded weird on the top floor, but now. I dunno, you're all spacy."

Once more, heat blooms through Ig's cheeks. She spins away from Verity before the woman can see the redness surely blushing her face. "Just tired." She begins walking, and soon enough Verity paces her.

"You don't have any military training or anything, do you?"

Ig shoots a look at her. "Why do you think that?"

"A hunch. But you don't seem as hardened like a soldier or even a mercenary. Not soft. Far from it. But, I dunno, there's just something different that separates you from the others here."

Ig is about to shrug when an alarm blares through the hall so loud she claps her hands to her ears. The lights flicker out and blue lights set in the floor turn on, giving the hall a gloomy, ethereal feel. Almost to the point of being disorientating. Meanwhile, the alarm continues to scream shrill insanity into her ears.

Verity leads Ig down the hall and around a corner to a door. Above the door it says Romus Room. Verity opens the door and shoved Ig inside.

There are no lights in the Romus Room, blue or otherwise. They're doused in utter darkness, but at least the alarm is muffled enough to think.

"What…what's going on?"

In the dark, Verity says, "I dunno. Maybe an attack."

"An *attack*? From who?"

But Verity doesn't respond.

Ig gapes at the darkness, not sure what to say or do, heart bashing itself against the walls of her chest. She brings her inhaler out and sucks down two puffs.

"You have asthma?"

Ig nods, then remembers Verity can't see it. "Yeah. Hate it."

"And Bracken still brought you on? What the hell was he thinking?"

"He asked me if I wanted to go. Said I could bow out with shame. But...I don't know. I just feel like I need to do this."

"You know there's no guarantee of getting paid, right?"

"I know."

Minutes stretch out like hours where neither say anything. The only sound is that of the alarm outside the room.

The door bursts open, filling the room with a ghostly blue glow. The alarm's blare batters into Ig's eardrums again.

"You two," a man silhouetted against the glow shouts over the alarm. "Follow me."

Verity grips Ig's forearm, leading her out of the room to where the man stands in the hallway. It's Bracken. His eyes are wide, and he keeps glancing over Ig's shoulder up the hall.

"Come on," he says finally. "We have a breach." Without explanation, he rushes down the hall.

Ig and Verity follow, Ig falling slightly behind. She's in shape. She's ran her entire life, especially during some jobs for Berkley. In short bursts, anyway. But, right now, it's like she's in some kind of fucked-up dream where she's wading through molasses and trying to run. Too slow. Too damn slow.

They take a right turn into not just hall but a wide corridor. The alarm is so loud, it's hard to focus on anything. Still, Ig follows the other two. She has no choice and it's the only thing her weary, stressed mind can cling to right now. The rest of the world is chaos. Madness wrapped in a ball of fear.

She shouldn't have gotten on the bus. She—

Bracken shoves open double doors and gestures for them to go through. He shut and locks the door. The alarm doesn't pierce those heavy doors and relief spills through Ig. Once more, her brain can function.

"Alright," Bracken says, a bit out of breath. "Are you two okay?"

"We're fine," Verity says. "What the hell is going on?"

He motions for them to follow as he hurries to a large space decked out with a honeycomb of gray cubicles. The place is entirely empty.

"Murdock," Bracken says. "He sent a team to infiltrate and destroy us."

"*What?*"

Bracken, glancing around, finally nods. "Seven I let in here took over Control. They killed the others. I don't know where Miles and Ash are."

"Shit," Verity says. "So, what are we gonna do?"

"What we planned. We kill the Mother of Monsters."

"But if Murdock has taken over Control...?" Verity, to Ig at least, appears so far on edge she might start throttling Bracken.

"Fake Control," Bracken says, leading them through the maze of cubicles. "They won't get far, but we gotta stay out of sight until they're taken care of."

"What are you saying?" Ig manages.

He stops and faces her. "This floor is a prop. Just in case of problems like this. People are coming to kill them right now."

"And if they don't?" Verity asks.

"They will," he says. "Below us is the real Resistance."

"How far down?" Ig asks, truly intrigued.

He shrugs. "As far down as it needs to be. Come on."

And that's that. He bustles away and it's all either Ig or Verity can do to keep up.

Not far from another set of double doors, the wall on the right explodes.

CHAPTER 6

Debris strikes Bracken, knocking him into the opposite wall, then all is consumed in a gray cloud of concrete dust.

Ig yanks Verity away just in time to avoid a large chunk of concrete, which crashes against the other wall and shatters into hundreds of pieces and more dust.

The air plumes with acrid dust and gods knew what else. Ig coughs, pulling Verity farther away from the blast. Verity struggles to be let go, but Ig refuses. They need to get away from all that dust. If she doesn't, having asthma might very well kill her.

Once at a reasonable distance, she lets Verity go.

The woman whirls on her. "He needs our help!"

Ig wants to tell her she can't go in with all that dust, but Verity doesn't wait. She watches Verity disappear into the gray cloud.

Someone shouts, "Mutts!"

Another person yells, "Take 'em out!"

And within all this are growls and a few roars.

What the hell is down here with us? Ig's mind reels with so many questions, which fuels more fear.

The chattering of gunfire severs all other thought. Ig hunkers behind a few cubicles and waits. There's nothing more she can do. Being the only one her mom can rely on for care, she needs to live. She needs to get through this for Mom. Even if Murdock's team besieges the compound, she needs to get out and take care of Mom. If she can't pay for a cure, then at least she'll be by Mom's side until the end.

The end.

It's something she doesn't want to even consider. A reality she tries to avoid, though it always sticks to the back of her mind like day-old bubble gum. Tacky, growing solid. Because, soon enough, Mom will get to the point where she can't swallow, let alone breathe on her own. It's this which plagues her mind daily. The realization she'll have to kill her mom when the time comes. It's a cold, bitter understanding. Mom refuses to have any care given to her. Once the breathing problems really begin…it's up to Ig to finally end it all for Mother.

The thought alone draws tears to her eyes every time. Even now.

How does one kill their own mother?

Ig angrily swipes away stray tears. She hates to feel so weak. So not in control.

Life isn't about control, though, she reminds herself. You can't control anything in life. Not entirely. As the world twirls on its axis, it doesn't give a damn about you. Because, like you, it's trying to survive. And it's a whole hell of a lot bigger.

Even so, she can't stop thinking about Mom. There must be a way to save her. And if Bracken is to be believed...she can. It's this hope which drives her more so than her own curiosity. Even a glimmer of hope is better than none. And in a world where hope is in limited supply like water and oil, she grips onto hers and refuses to let go.

Eventually, the gunfire ceases. She waits, listening. Despite the small crashes of falling debris, the place falls into a stupor of silence. She tries to quell the thudding of her heart, for fear of being heard. A silly thought that, but she imagines the pounding drawing attention. Attention she doesn't want.

Minutes crawl by. Sweat squiggles down her face, cutting clean grooves through the grime.

Holding her breath, Ig inches to the edge of the cubicle and peers around the corner. Her gaze meets a pair of black-clad knees. She looks up to find an older man with a harsh, pink scar cut diagonally across his dower, heavily lined face. His bald head gleams, despite the lack of true lighting.

A crooked grin splits that weathered, scared face. "Hey, Kitty. On your feet."

From behind the man, people whoop and holler. Ig, trembling, tries to stand, but can't find the strength.

He bends, hooks hand under her collar, and yanks her up. Gripping her shirt, he draws her closer to him, almost eye-level. Cold, blue eyes, whites streaked in tiny, red veins. The madness practically bakes off him.

"Ah, I was wonderin' when I'd come across one of you people," he says, voice so low it might as well have been a growl.

"Please," she wheezes. Proverbial steel bands around her chest cinch tighter and tighter.

"What ya got there, Corb?" another man shouts.

A scrawny man, around Ig's age, peeks around Corb's broad shoulder. His eyes are buggy, shifting sporadically in their thin sockets. He gives her a full-on grin and she's not really surprised to see most of his teeth are missing.

Corb chuckles, shoves Ig backward. She stumbles over something and falls hard on her butt. Pain shoots up her back.

"Got ourselves a true savage, boys." Corb draws a large hunting knife from the sheath on his belt and smiles. "Think we got some scalpin' to do."

Three other men crowded behind Corb. One of them mutters, "That's not part of the mission, Corb."

His grin drops. He spins, grabs the man who spoke, and tosses him. The man crashes into a stand of cubicles, rebounds, and draws a sidearm. So fluid, this man's movements are. He's shorter than Corb, wiry, but there's something more in his eyes. A strength Corb doesn't possess.

Corb grunts, extends his arms, spreading wide. "Think ya got what it takes, Telly? Go ahead. Do it, boy."

Gun still aimed at Corb, Telly says, "We have our orders, man. This isn't a free-for-all killing spree."

Ig, slowly, scoots away from the men. If she can get to the door, maybe she can make a run for it.

The other three men laugh. The bug-eyed one spouts, "'fraid of a lil savage, are ya, Telly?"

Telly shoots a glint of hate at the scrawny man. "We only have an hour to infiltrate and seize the chip. If we fail, Murdock will personally hang us. You know that."

This stops all of them for a moment. Even Corb.

Then another of the men says, "She's just a savage. Murdock won't care." And Ig instantly recognizes him. It's an older man from the beach. The one with the faded, red hat.

"It's not about that," Telly says. "It's about infiltrating and seizing the chip. That's why we were sent in place of the real people Bracken thought he rounded up. We infiltrate. We get the chip and files. We get out. That is our mission. Not killing every living thing within a ten-mile radius."

Ig continues scooting away until her back bumps against the double doors. No one appears to notice.

Corb nods. "Yup. But we might as well have a bit of fun, right?"

All but Telly mutter praise.

After a few seconds, Telly straightens and smiles. "Guess you're right. Let's waste her."

The men turn toward Ig just as she's standing and pressing the door latch down.

Bug-eyes titters. "Lookit her. Thinks she can run."

Corb, crooked grin resurfacing, says, "Well, let's see show her how far she'll run." He starts forward—

It happens quickly. Three quick pops.

Corb is the last to fall, though not before focusing a glare on Telly. He opens his mouth, but only blood comes out. On his knees, he looks at Ig and the hatred in his light, blue eyes sinks all the way to her spirit.

Telly steps away from the cubicle, shoves Corb down, and puts a bullet into the back of his head. He holsters his gun and gives Corb a kick in the ribs. Corb doesn't move. Satisfied, Telly turns his attention to Ig.

She's opening the doors to run, when he says, "I'm from the Resistance."

This stops her, even though her brain is screaming at her to run. She's about to do so anyway, but then a more familiar voice behind her sounds.

"Ignia. It's okay."

Verity?

Ig thought she died with Bracken in the dust cloud. Maybe shot by the deranged men. And yet...

She turns around and her heart fills a little. Standing behind Telly, Bracken gives a smile and a small salute. Verity just smiles.

"Well, then," Telly says after a moment. He glances from Ig to Bracken and Verity. "How about we get this mission going, eh?" He gives Bracken a pat on the shoulder as he passes. "I'll have Rick and Thom clean the mess up. You three better come with me."

CHAPTER 7

No one speaks as Telly leads the way through the ruination of the hall where the intruders went berserk, all the way to the end of the hall. A wall of reflective tiles.

There are no other halls branching from this main one.

"Um," Verity says, glancing around. "It's a dead end."

Telly winks. "We haven't been hidden for so long because we're stupid." He presses a hand on an octagon-shaped tile. With all the reflections, Ig would've never noticed it.

A small beep, and the wall whispers into the ceiling. Beyond the threshold, a long corridor stretches, steadily sloping downward. There aren't any doors. Nothing but polished steel walls, black-tiled floor, and ceiling.

"Welcome to Hell," Bracken says and shoots a grin at everyone.

Telly sighs, shakes his head, and tweezes the bridge of his nose with the index finger and thumb of his right hand. "Man, I swear, your jokes get lamer and lamer every damn day."

"Oh, you're just jealous I can tell a joke." Bracken nods at Verity. "It was funny, right?"

Verity rolls her eyes. "Uh…sure?"

He claps his hands. "Ha! See?"

Telly makes an *ugh* sound and walks away, once more shaking his head.

"Oh, come on," Bracken says, smiling at Ig. "It was a little funny, right?"

Ig snorts. "It's funny that you think it's funny."

Verity chuckles. "Holy shit, she speaks!"

Bracken laughs, and together they descend into a mirrored abyss while the secret wall slides back in place behind them.

***

Ig isn't sure how long it takes them to finally come to a T-intersection of the corridor, but long enough to wonder if it'll go on forever.

Telly goes left and like the main corridor, this one slopes downward.

It doesn't take long before they come to a set of heavy double doors. Here, Telly says, "Teller Sullivan. Open."

A series of clicks echo throughout the corridor.

With a hiss of escaping air, the doors swing open of their own accord, giving way to a massive room filled with bustling people and aglow with monitors.

Before they enter, Verity grabs Telly's arm. "So, you were with the group too?"

He grunts. "Can't let Bracken here go out without a leash, right?"

"Hey…dickhead," Bracken spouts. "Who co-founded this damn Resistance?"

Telly, chuckling, waves a dismissive hand. "Yeah, yeah. Let's go."

Bracken lets loose a heavy sigh and gestures for Verity and Ig to go ahead of him.

The room is so huge, Ig can't tell where it ends, if it ever does. Other than the glow of literally thousands of computer monitors, there are no lights. People dash this way and that, so many, it feels impossible. And yet…here they are.

Hundreds of voices speaking almost in unison turns maddening until Telly says, "The expected group number is considerably smaller, but Leon no doubt wishes to proceed."

"Where's Miles and Ash?" Bracken asks.

Ig blinks. Gods, she almost forgot about those two.

"Leon almost predicted this," Telly says. "Follow me."

"Meeting Hall?" Bracken sidles up beside Telly.

"Recreation Room," Telly replies.

Behind these men, Ig frowns. She's having not second thoughts, but third thoughts. Something feels incredibly off, despite knowing she's in the Resistance's company. Corruption, sometimes, slithers in on both sides. Blue. Red. For corruption, it doesn't matter. Money changes everything, even morals and common sense.

Eventually, all the way across the room, they stop at a glass door. Here, Telly faces all of them. "Do not look Leon directly in the eye. Be respectful." With this, he opens the door.

Ig, Verity, and Bracken enter a highly lit room. A stark contrast compared to the cavernous room with all the monitors and bustling people.

Already seated at the table are Miles and Ash, along with a few others Ig doesn't recognize. At the head of the room, a small woman stands, brunette hair buzzed short. Her bronzed face rests in an ambiguous state.

Telly sits at the far end of the table while Bracken takes a seat near the head. Verity shrugs and sits across from Ash. Ig sits across from Miles.

The woman at the front of the room doesn't move, nor does her expression change. She simply stares at the small group, unflinching.

"You just survived an attempted infiltration," the woman says, voice even. For the first time, she moves, stepping across the room to a large monitor. Ash and Mile have to turn to see. "What you experienced is exactly our foolproof way of singling them out. Once inside, they simply can't help themselves. They attack, and we're always ready." She glances at Ig and Verity. "The two here now from this recent group, you have been cleared."

Verity appears on the verge of saying something, but clamps her mouth shut.

Be respectful were the last words Telly told them.

So be it.

"No," the woman says, "let me introduce myself. I'm Leon Gates. Leader of this rebellion and co-founder of the Resistance." He points at Bracken, not far from her. "Bracken is my other half in this. We make decisions together."

Bracken grunts. "You just have a better way with words is all."

And, for the first time, Leon reveals a sliver of emotion. A smile quirks her lips. "Uh-huh. Brains too. But who's counting…" Her gaze flicks to Ig and the others. "You're all here for a reason. We're going to kill the Mother of Monsters. If we want to save our seas, it's the only way. She's a product of an evolving world, though her very presence is altering ours. The more beasts she births, the more the oceans starve. And if I was the superstitious type, I might believe the Devil's Trench created her out of spite."

Miles straightens. "The Devil's Trench?"

"It's the longest, widest trench in the Pacific Ocean," Leon says. "Although, you won't find it on the Internet, nor in any book. It's a trench only known to a few people and branches of military." She winks. "It's also said to be a portal to Hell."

Ig had heard stories about the Devil's Trench. None of them good and all telling of demons and evil creatures leaking into our world over time.

She never believed those stories. Until now…

No one says anything, so Leon taps the monitor. It lights up, revealing at first an image much like the one Bracken showed the larger group in the beginning. Only difference is the quality. Here, Ig can actually see features of the monstrous thing being called "The Mother of Monsters." And it's massive. A sprawling, green and black mass almost as large as Greenland before the Atlantic swallowed it up.

Ig blinks, squints, making sure she's really seeing what's on the big monitor.

"There is no name for her," Leon says, her face neutral. "She's a species all her own. And we have serious reason to believe she's the result of all the mutated monsters out there. From the Leviathan, to Jörmungandr, and, perhaps, even the *Dunkleosteus*. There's one man threading all these together, though. Murdock Jones. We have reason to believe he's on the hunt for Mother. From intercepted comms, we've found he's planning an invasion on Europe and the Middle East. Being in control of literal monsters will decimate his competition. He's been working on this for a very long time."

Out of nowhere, Verity says, "For oil?"

Leon's face never changes. "That's part of it." She taps the monitor. "But it's more about water, now." The image on the screen reveals an intricate system running through the world, all squiggly deep blue lines like varicose veins. "Murdock has switched his interests from oil to water, seeing as one is scarcer than the other nowadays."

"What's that got to do with Mother?" Miles asks.

Leon nods. Another indication she's human. "A fair enough question. You see, Murdock loves his oil. He builds his fortune around it, but now water is in greater demand. He wants to be the hero to people so they support him. It's one of the oldest tricks. That's his main focus. Water. His secondary focus is on Mother. He wants her DNA. He wants to play God and create his own monstrous offspring. We have word he has already deployed a team to retrieve the DNA. This, we can't let happen. If he gets hold of such information, the world will finally fall under his reign."

A woman seated beside Miles shrugs. "Like the world can get any worse. I mean, it's already falling."

Leon favors the woman with a small smile. "And we're here to reverse that. Or at least stop it. Point is, if Murdock gets his way, a lot more people will die than during the climate shifts and second Civil War. We're talking near global genocide."

The woman huffs out a breath, leans back in her chair. She lowers her head and Ig can't help but feel for her. The world is crumbling, but some evil man out there doesn't care. He wants it to die. But why?

"Ash?" Leon says. "You have some information to share?"

Ash stands and steps to the front of the room. Leon moves away from the large monitor. He taps an icon on the screen, revealing what is now being called Mother. The monster creating monster offspring. Just below the surface.

"When Bracken first let me see this image weeks ago, I thought it was fake. Nothing natural looks like this, nor gives birth to mythical *and* prehistoric marine life. It's just not possible. Or so I thought until it was captured by a drone breaching the surface for a few seconds." He taps another icon and Ig's heart stutters. For the first time, she's staring into the amber eyes of a thing that should not be. Into the eyes of madness itself.

Ash clears his throat and faces the small group. "I was wrong. It's real. And we also have reason to believe Murdock wants its DNA specifically to not only destroy humanity but create his own race. Like Leon pointed out, he wants to play God."

"But you guys don't know all of this for sure, right?" Verity asks. "Unless—"

"We have tapped into a lot of comms and emails over the past few weeks," Bracken says. "A couple were conversations about killing off every living thing on earth and establishing a new race. Murdock wanted this even when I met him. We thought we were out there to help fix an old oil rig. He knew about the Leviathan. He purposely sabotaged the mission so only one would make it out. Lieutenant Ramses. She was meant to collect a sample of the Leviathan and leave us all there to die." He grunts. "Problem with that, though—she was completely insane."

Bracken leans forward, clasping his hands on the table before him. "I was a fool and lead my entire crew, my friends, to their death."

"Murdock is manipulative," Leon says, placing a hand on Bracken's shoulder. "And you were desperate. You were lost and thought you found a way out of the darkness."

He nods, frowns at his hands, though doesn't say anything.

"Okay," Miles says. "So, we kill this thing. What's to stop him from collecting samples from the dead body?"

Leon gives Ash a nod, and he returns to his seat.

She stands front and center again. "This operation will be a massive undertaking. You are the dispatch crew. Another crew will follow behind to ensure the corpse is destroyed."

"So," Ig says, and hates the feel of all the eyes shifting toward her. "Why am I here? I'm not a monster hunter. I was never in the military. All I did before this is steal rare items and harvest delicacies from the sea."

Leon's face softens. "Ignia, correct?"

"Yeah."

The small woman smiles, and this too is soft. Gentle. Kindness shines from her eyes. "Your role is the most important."

A frown works its way across Ig's face. "It is?" Her gaze drifts from Leon to Bracken. He's also smiling. "Okay, you guys are really starting to weird me out now."

Leon chuckles and clasps her hands behind her back. "There's one reason, and one reason only you accepted to join us on this operation. Your mother, am I correct? To pay for a cure, Bracken informed me."

Ig glances around the room. "Yeah. But there's no guarantee. I guess I'm hoping this will pay out."

"Of course," Leon says. "But what if there's another way to save your mother?"

"What are you saying?" Ig almost slams a fist down in frustration.

"Ig," Bracken says, "The Mother is an anomaly. She can breed all kinds of creatures and well…Ash?"

Ash smiles, nods at Ig. "With its uniqueness, it may carry a cure for cancers of all kinds. AIDS." He holds Ig's gaze. "Even ALS."

Her heart gives a slow thud. She shakes her head, sure she heard him wrong. "What?"

Ash shrugs. "It's not conclusive, of course. Like the money, there's no real guarantee. But this is what the scientists are saying, and I trust them."

"The scientists?"

"We have our own scientists here, Ignia," Leon says. "Some of the top in their fields."

There are no words. Can it be true? A real cure from such a monster? A way to truly save Mom?

"Your job," Bracken says, "is to take plasma samples from various sections of the creature. That's it. You'll be doing what you do best. Stealing and harvesting. And the results might very well not only save your mother, but millions of others as well."

Tears prickle her eyes. She stares at the table.

A hand slowly, gently rubs her back. In her ear is Leon's soothing voice. "That's what we're all about. More so than anything else. Saving people. This is why we're the Resistance. You have the most important role to play here, dear Ignia."

Ig sniffs, wipes a tear from the tip of her nose before it drips onto the table. "Then let's do it."

The hand slips away from her back. The rest of the meeting commences, though Ig's mind fixes on Mom. Finally, a pinprick of light at the end of a long, dark tunnel.

CHAPTER 8

The frill shark hasn't eaten days.

It struggles. Fighting for its miserable life, as all things on this Godforsaken planet are doing. Fighting, though to what end? When do they all realize their time is up?

He runs a manicured thumb along a bleach-white forehead. Anna's skull. It's been years since he lost his daughter to a stomach tumor. Too many years. Years of searching sampling. All for her. If he can splice her DNA with something compatible…maybe he can have her back again.

If not her, at least someone comparable to her. A twin, of sorts.

Murdock Jones leans back in his crushed velvet chair, watching the frill shark try to eat and coming up short every time. The pressure in the tank isn't right, but he refuses to adjust it. He wants to witness for himself how long a thing will fight for its life until finally giving up. Not because he necessarily wants to but must. He's watched many things die over the years. Humans included. All experiments.

He swirls aged scotch in a crystal glass and takes a sip. Long gone is the pleasurable burn trickling down his throat. The heat of the alcohol. Ah, but the taste. Notes of coffee, berries, and something almost citrus.

The frill shark has, so far, lasted ten days like this. Lower pressure and more light than it's used to. Even with the rest of the room shrouded in darkness, there's too much light. There is plenty of food in the tank, but the shark is just too weak to eat. It won't be long now…

"Mr. Jones?"

He stiffens in the chair, unaware of the interloper. "Yes?"

"News of our agents."

Murdock sips his scotch. "A successful infiltration, I presume?"

The man behind him pauses a moment. "No. There's been no communication since the beach. We believe they were discovered."

Murdock sighs. "And why do you believe this, Nathan?"

"Well, there hasn't been any communication for several hours, Mr. Jones. The mission was supposed to be complete by now."

"And," Murdock says, swirling his drink, "what if they got tied up? Maybe they're in hiding and just waiting until all is clear. Did we at least track where the Resistance's bunker is?"

"No, sir. The signal was blocked at the beach."

He's not one for anger, but now…

Murdock shoots out of the chair, spins, and chucks the glass at Nathan. The boy ducks it without much effort.

"They've been intercepting our comms and you can't even track our people? What the hell do you people do? I pay you enough, better be doing something."

Nathan, hands at his sides, nods. "There's a counter-mission in place. But, sir, I should add we have four teams already in route to our main objective. If all goes well, we'll be the first to reach the creature."

Murdock's anger eases. "Is that so?"

"Yes, Mr. Jones. Sixteen hours before contact."

A long breath, too heavy to be a sigh, flows out of Murdock's mouth. He waves a hand at Nathan. "Good. Keep me updated on all that."

He's about to sit when Nathan adds, "Sir?"

His temples thrum. "For Christ sake, Nathan, what?"

The boy, no older than twenty-five, stands firm. Murdock likes that. A kid with some steel in him. Unlike his last assistant, Christopher. Little weasely bastard would flinch at a butterfly.

"We have collected some profiles for a few among this latest group. Do you wish to see the files?"

Murdock smiles. Yes, he likes this boy. "Send them through."

Nathan gives a bit of a bow, turns, and walks toward the door, polished black shoes clicking along a polished, black floor.

"Nathan?"

The boy stops and faces Murdock.

"Good work."

Nathan's blank expression never falters. "Thank you, Mr. Jones." He gives another small bow and leaves the room.

The door swings shut with a clunk. The sound echoes throughout Murdock's large chamber.

There was a time when he loved the sound. Reminded him of giant castles and powerful kings and daring knights…maybe even a dragon or two.

Now, however, the sound only reminds him of how alone he really is. The clunk of a dying heart in an empty chest. Dark and alone.

Forgotten…

Murdock absently strokes his perfectly trimmed, black mustache. Well, with the dye it's black. Under the façade, the dark hair has become dusted with salt. Silvery gray strands also swim below the black dye on his head.

A façade.

Has that really what he's become? Fifty years of ruling the oil trades and practically owning much of America…for what? What's wealth if there's no one else to share it with?

He must get that big mother's DNA.

For Anna.

Murdock turns to the tank, blinks. The frill shark floats belly up while what's supposed to be its prey nibbles chunks out of the corpse. Funny how tables turn so quickly.

He pours himself some more scotch, lifts the glass to the dead shark. "You fought well, my friend."

He knocks the scotch back. Heat fills him, and he doesn't feel quite so alone. But it only lasts a moment. The shadows grow, coiling in like a massive serpent. A tear rolls down his pallid cheek.

Shadows are shadows. There's nothing here but emptiness.

CHAPTER 9

"Again," Miles says and steps behind her.

Ig breathes deep and sprints forward. She jabs the five-foot-long spike into the first pig carcass, spins, stabs it into a second. She yanks the spike out, sidesteps and jumps into a pool. Everything becomes a disorientated mess of bubbles and the alien roars of being underwater.

She forgot the goggles.

Shit.

Still, through all the bubbles, she spots her target and swims toward it. Unlike before, she keeps her pace steady. The saltwater stings her eyes though, and she has to close them for a moment. Then all is roaring darkness. She counts to five and opens her eyes again.

The target isn't far.

Lungs burning for air, she kicks faster, spike held like a jousting lance. Not far from the target, she lunges—

Something black crashes into her, driving out what little air in her lungs she has. She fights not to draw in a breath. The thing wrestles with her until she gives the signal she needs air. In a matter of seconds, she's hauled upward. The moment her head breaches the surface she sucks in a breath.

The thing that struck her underwater isn't a thing at all, but a man. One of the master divers of the group, Nihal Warren, pulls her to the side of the pool.

"Better this time," he says, helping her out.

She coughs, still trying to breathe, though manages a nod and thumbs up as she rolls onto her back outside the pool.

A pair of goggles clacks on the floor beside her. "Forgot those."

She glances at Miles, his face drawn in something bordering disapproval and bemusement.

Ig coughs, takes a few breaths. "Lost the spike too." She rolls, chest tightening and hating herself for just now noticing. "Get my...inhaler."

But he doesn't move. Instead, he takes a knee beside her. "There won't be any inhalers in the mech."

She frowns at him and tries to crawl away. He pulls her back, holds her ankle.

"Control your breathing, Ig. In through the nose, out through the mouth. Slow and easy."

"That...shit...don't work."

"Well, it better, otherwise you can't go on this mission."

Never in all her life has she hated someone like she does Miles right now. She kicks, fighting his hold on her.

"Bracken," Miles shouts. "Need you here."

Bracken kneels beside her. "Just relax, Ig. Listen to Miles. He's a decorated Navy Seal. He knows about these things."

"In through the nose, out through the mouth," Miles repeats. "I once had a guy who somehow made it into Seals training with asthma. This is how we got him through the training. Because, when you're out there, an inhaler won't always be available. You need to program your body how to survive."

Ig wants to punch him and Bracken and tell them all to get bent. She wants to grab her inhaler and just go and—

"Do you want to save your mom?" Bracken asks.

This ignites a fire inside her. She swivels, planting her heel into the side of Mile's face. She shoves Bracken away, crawls a bit, and manages to stand. Her inhaler rests on a green bench not far.

But…she stops.

Glaring at the inhaler, she draws in a slow breath and blows it out just as slowly. Controlled. She coughs a couple times as she restarts her lungs. She never stops breathing in through the nose and out the mouth. This has never worked for her before.

And yet, as she continues, she finds herself breathing fairly regular. Not quite top notch, but close enough to stave off the panic. The wheezing eases, finally disappearing.

A large hand gently massages her shoulder. "Hell of a kick you got." Miles chuckles. "And now, we'll make you a Seal yet. This is controlled breathing. You're doing better than most. Now, I want you to try the course again, without using the inhaler first."

She doesn't hate him, even if she wants to. He's right. He's teaching her not to be so dependent on the inhaler.

"Okay," she says, and faces him. "Where's the spike?"

Miles places a new one in her hand, nods. She nods back and turns to the small course he set up for her training. She doesn't say it, but in her mind, she shouts, "Oo-Rah!"

***

Ig downs a bottle of water and shovels some casserole into her mouth. She doesn't care what it is. All she knows is the hunger and thirst. Hours spent in training has left her so drained she just doesn't care about anything but food and water.

Once the meal is finished, however, she sits, trying to keep her eyes open while the others chat among themselves. Weariness settles over her like a gray, weighted blanket. Her mind fills with soft fuzz like goose down.

"Let's get you to bed." Verity? Yes. The beautiful girl with a will like iron. Or something.

Someone helps Ig to her feet, helping her walk. Her crutch. Not Verity. Bracken? Miles? Ash? A man, maybe, for the one helping her along is much taller than Verity.

Her sight glazes over and still she fights sleep. She needs to stay awake for just a bit longer. At least until they get her to her room and—

"Load her up in the sub," a familiar voice says. Leon? "She can sleep there. We just pinged two of Murdock's teams heading for the target. They're eight hours ahead of us."

Verity says, "We'll never catch them."

The person holding her, voice deeper and definitely a man, says, "The sub has an offset for hyperdrive. Never been used, though. Not sure of the test results either."

"Make it work," Leon says. "I'll deploy the second team as soon as you're…"

Ig can't fight it anymore. Sleep, dark and silent, washes over her. It caresses her into oblivion.

She knows no more.

***

It's a dream. She knows it's a dream. And yet, this doesn't stop the terror gripping her.

"You left me," Mom says. She's in her bed, stained with piss and shit. "You left me with *her*."

Ig tries to say something, but her lips are sewn shut.

The woman who's supposed to be taking care of Mom walks into the room and slaps Mom across the face.

Ig tries to move, but she can't. She's stuck to the wall like a fly in a honey.

The woman dips a teaspoon into what appears to be applesauce and shoves it into Mom's mouth. Mom sputters as this vile woman shovels more and more applesauce into her mouth.

Ig cries out to stop, but the woman won't stop. She keeps shoveling and shoveling. Applesauce glops from Mom's mouth. The evil woman keeps—

***

Ig wakes to a gradual lull, a scream caught in her throat like a rusty fishhook.

She swallows and rolls onto her side, not liking the bobbing and odd rocks.

When her eyes finally open, she stares a Verity directly across from her. The woman is asleep in a stable pod. When Ig sits, she finds she's the only one not in a pod.

She also spots Bracken, Miles, Ash, and the others. Everyone at the meeting except for Leon is in slender, white pods. But, if everyone is asleep, who's steering the boat? Or sub? Whatever.

Ig sits on a makeshift cot, letting herself get used to the motion. She's never been seasick before, but right then...she just isn't sure. Her stomach lurches with every rise, dip, and shift. Her head pulses, threatening a migraine.

She glances up and down the corridor she finds herself in. Save for the pods, benches, pipes, and a couple gauges, it's empty. To the left, about twenty feet away, is a closed metal door. To the right lay only darkness.

Standing proves to be the most difficult task she's ever attempted. She plops onto the cot more than once until she figures out a way to keep the rocking sensation from robbing Ig of her balance. She latches onto a set of green tubes running along the walls until her balance figures out what the hell it's doing.

Once everything equalizes, she makes her way toward the closed door. Which is oddly also a difficult task. Feels like she's walking directly into gale force winds, boots sloshing through six inches of molasses. She pushes on, struggling against whatever force is pushing back. Not far from the door, another of those white pods sits, this one empty.

Why is there an empty pod? And why is it so far away from the others?

It's mine, she thinks. *Why am I not in it, though?*

Another few steps and she's at the door, gripping the latch. She's about to open it when Leon's voice says, "You were taken out of your pod, so you could wake up before the others. I need you to sit and pull the harness down. The ride is going to get bumpy soon."

Ig glances around until she spots a camera tucked in the rounded corner not far from her pod, overlooking the entire corridor, or whatever she's standing in. A bay? Something like that.

"Why do I need to be awake first?"

"Please sit and buckle in, Ignia. We're traveling in warp to beat Murdock's teams to Mother and the Devil's Trench. If we should need to slow down or stop suddenly and you're not buckled in…well, I'm sure you can figure it out."

She does and quickly finds a seat. The harness is like something one might find on a fighter jet. She buckles into the seat.

"Good," Leon says. "Now, you were woken up earlier because you need time to prep."

Ig blinks. "Prep?"

"At the rear of the bay is a mech. You know what a mech is, correct? Surely Miles and Bracken trained you?"

Heart skipping a beat, she frowns. "They trained me some, but not in a mech."

A long pause follows. Then, "Instructions have been uploaded to the mech. Once we're clear of turbulence, I want you to get into the mech and seal yourself in. Don't worry, it's self-sustaining. You'll never run out of air."

"That's supposed to make me feel better?" she spouts without thinking.

"Yes," Leon says, undeterred. "The mech is designed by Bracken himself. Nothing like the sleek one he used to battle the Leviathan. This one is heavily armored as well as versatile. Instructions will be available on how to operate it as soon as you're sealed inside. Voice activated. In the right arm is the collection needle. You need to collect as much blood as you can from its brain, heart, and torso. There is also an option for tissue sampling. If you can, cut out some skin. The more we have, the better we can save lives and—"

The world turns to jostling, quaking madness. Ig grips the straps of her harness as pressure inside the bay increases. She bounces out of her seat before hovering inches above it. Forces yank her in every direction. Her back slams into the seat. Her chest presses into the harness. Pain slices through her from top to bottom as she tossed around like a ragdoll, even in the harness.

There's no room to scream. No breaths to hold. The brutal assault destroys everything in her mentally and physically. Stirs everything up like a mindless stew. One second, vomiting seems likely, the next…it feels as if the very air has fists and is beating her relentlessly.

It all ends just as quickly as it began, leaving Ig grunting in pain and fighting a tightening asthma attack. Luckily, someone was thinking and put the inhaler in her pocket. She pulls it out now and sucks down two puffs, holding her breath for a few seconds. When she blows the final breath out, relief spills through her. She's somewhere between euphoria and pain when the medicine takes hold.

Her stomach, on the other hand, continues to roll like a green, greasy ball. She fights vomiting all over herself. Once this goes away, she's left with only the aches and pains of all the chaos.

"The rough waters are behind us now," Leon says through wherever the speakers are. "Get into the mech. Seal it. I uploaded further instructions. Once we're close to Mother, you will be deployed. Gather the samples and return to the sub. The others will keep her distracted. If in danger, the mech also has weapons. Use them at your own discretion."

Still reeling from what Leon calls turbulence, Ig unbuckles the harness and practically falls out of the seat. Her legs are like pillars of gelatin. She manages to stand upright and make her way toward the rear of the bay.

A mech? Yeah, she's never been in one. Never really considered the things useful. Or if they were useful, it was for war, not other things. The very thought of being confined in one scared her more than a little. What if it malfunctions and never lets her out? She's read of such stories where a mech will just shut down and people die inside them. The horror of it kept her away for years, even if Berkley said to give a mech a try one time.

Now, that very fear crawls over her skin and scuttles up her spine like foreboding, black spiders.

It doesn't take her long to find the mech.

How would she not?

The thing is huge. At least nine feet tall. So much larger than the mechs she read about, which are nearly form fitting. More like exoskeletons. This, however…this is something different. Sleek in design, but at the same time hulking and intimidating. A thing of beauty and destruction.

It takes more than a few trials and errors to figure out how to open the damn thing. Because it's voice activated, she gives it a try.

"Open?"

A sharp hiss severs her thoughts and the mech's top hatch opens. Metal rungs slip out of the mech's surface along one leg, providing a ladder to the hatch. She grabs a rung, but hesitates. Fears swirl through her mind. All the possibilities of doom rest upon her shoulders. What would her mother think? What would Mother do?

For as far back as Ig can remember, Mom has been the very image of strength. Absent of a father, Ig learned everything from Mom. How to chop down a tree. How to split wood. How to take care of livestock, hunt, butcher pigs, chickens, and deer. Weaving baskets and minor blacksmithing, all incorporated. Plus, academics along the way. Mom did it all.

That's why it hurts seeing her so weak and frail.

Now, though, that's just how Ig feels. Weak and frail as she climbs into the mech and eases herself into a small seat. The hatch slips shut without her speaking a word, jolting her heart into overdrive. She takes another quick puff from her inhaler, just in case.

She stares out a curved window. Complete one-eighty degrees. Inside the mech, only her breathing keeps her company. It's like sitting in a steel box. Hollow, yet suffocating. A hiss fills the mech, cool air rushes around her, and all at once the suffocating sensation vanishes. More like sitting in a car now, which is a relief and—

"Hello."

Ig sucks in a breath, frowns, glances around. "Uh, hi?"

"Welcome to Battle Mech Sully-3. This is a tutorial of operations. Sully-3 is the most advanced compact Battle Mech available, designed and programmed by Bracken Tull. The programming of this particular mech has been altered to mission parameters. Thrust speeds have been increased by sixty knots. To apply thruster speeds and directions, simply say: Forward thrust (any speed), left or right side thrust (gradual speed), and up and down (any speed). To have motion sensors activated, say so now."

She blinks. "Motion sensors?"

"On or off?"

"On."

"Motion sensors are on. Do you wish to walk?"

This thing is so strange but doesn't seem too difficult to operate. So far, anyway. "Yes."

"Okay. Say: Walk. Then say: Walk, jog, run, or sprint."

"Walk, walk," she says and all the lights and monitors in the mech winks on. It moves forward, lumbering toward the pods where Verity, Bracken, Miles, Ash, and the others still sleep.

"To stop walking, simply say, Stop."

"Stop," Ig says. The mech slows to a stop.

"After this tutorial, please buckle into the unit using the harness provided. Now…let's begin the weapon and DNA collection tutorials."

Ig sighs, intrigued, but just wanting to get this all over with.

She's somewhere in the middle of collecting DNA samples when the mech's sensors detect an outside alarm.

CHAPTER 10

"...sir."

Murdock jolts awake in his chair in front of the tank. There's nothing more than bones left of the frill shark.

A hand falls on his shoulder. He grabs it, heart slamming in his throat, twists—

"Mr. Jones, it's me. Nathan. Sir!" Pain taints his voice, making it a bit more shrill than normal.

Murdock shoves the hand away and stands, heart a frantic mess in his chest. His vision swims and he curses himself for hitting the scotch too hard.

There was a time when he refused to drink.

Nowadays though...

"What the hell do you want?" His voice is rough and slurred, and he hates the sound of it.

"Sorry to disturb you, Mr. Jones, but I have an update."

He really can't focus on anything through the blur of scotch, but he tries. "What?"

"Mr. Tull's team of the Resistance slipped by our teams. Our people were ordered immediately to seek and destroy by Captain Sullivan."

"And?" He rests a hand on the high-backed chair to stabilize his balance.

"They disappeared on us, sir. The teams are tracking, though."

"I want them alive," Murdock says, surprising himself. "Don't destroy their vessel."

For the first time, Nathan shows a sliver of emotion. A tiny crease between his blue eyes. "How do we capture them, sir?"

Murdock pulls the gun from the shoulder holster and buries a bullet into Nathan's brain. He watches the boy's body drop to the floor, nerves twitching until they too finally die.

"How do we capture them...?" Murdock repeats Nathan. "I'll tell you how we capture them, asshole. We net them once they leave the sub they're in." He gives Nathan's body a healthy kick in the ribs. "We fucking *wait*."

Nathan, very much dead, says nothing.

Once Murdock's rage subsides into blurry drunkenness, he stumbles to his desk. He misses the monstrosity at first, running headlong into a shelf of books he hasn't touched since Anna was born. An old tome of Moby Dick thumped to the polished, black floor.

"Drunk," he mutters, then snorts.

He kicks the heavy book aside and faces his massive desk. After a few trials and errors, he finds his way to the phone and calls Captain Sullivan directly.

"Sir?" Sullivan answers on the second ring.

"Do not destroy the Resistance's vessel. Wait for them to deploy, then net them. Haul them aboard and sedate them. I want them alive."

There's a long pause. "Sir, with all due respect, if we let them—"

"No one dies this time, understand? If they're in trouble, try to protect them. Capture them and bring them to me."

Another long pause. "What about the DNA samples, sir?"

Murdock's gaze shifts to the side. DNA samples? What the hell is he...oh...?

"Yeah, um, get those too."

"Are you feeling alright, Mr. Jones?"

He ruffles. "Of course, Captain. See to it orders are followed through."

"Copy that," Captain Sullivan says.

"Oh, Sullivan?"

"Yes, sir?"

"I'll need a new assistant. Nathan is kind of...dead."

Once more, the long pause. Then, "Very well. I will send a crew in to dispose of the body and assign a new assistant."

"See that you do, Sullivan. I'll be in my inner chambers resting."

"Copy, sir. Out."

Murdock taps the End call icon and staggers away from the main chamber to the smaller inner chamber. He shuts the door behind him and falls into bed. The world beings to spin...

Then he knows no more.

CHAPTER 11

"Communications translate this submarine has been hit," the dull voice of the mech says.

"Oh, lovely," Ig manages while she refrains from breaking open the pods to wake the others up.

"Do you wish to counter-attack?"

One of her eyebrows lift. "I can do that?"

"Sully-3 is synced to the vessel's systems per default. Do you wish to counter-attack?"

Ig shrugs. "Sure."

"Targets locked. Firing laser bursts in three, two, one…"

The outside alarm falls silent. The pods do not open. For a time, Ig drifts into relief.

The mech's tutorial was a lot of common sense stuff, but good to know, especially when she has to be out there collecting the samples.

That's if whoever is attacking doesn't destroy Leon's sub first, of course.

"Direct hit," the mech says. "Do you wish to fire again?"

"Damage?" Ig ventures, not really sure what to expect.

"Enemy vessel has received major damage. They may fire in response, though are taking on gallons of water as we speak."

"Maintain course," Ig says.

"ETA, one hour to target."

Five minutes later, the white pods open.

Another five minutes and everyone begins waking up. Verity is the first to sit and glance around. Her gaze fixes on Ig and the mech for a long time. Then she shakes her head and crawls out of the pod.

In no more than six minutes, three others climb out of their pods. Three Ig hasn't met yet.

Following the initial three are the other people she's been waiting for climb out. Bracken, Miles, and Ash.

All of them, still obviously sleepy, face her. One of the other three, a man somewhere in his late forties, maybe, draws his sidearm. He starts forward, but Bracken stops him.

Through the mech's speakers, Ig catches some of the conversation.

"She's one of us," Bracken says. "Put that damn thing away."

The man glances from Bracken to Ig. "No one told me there'd be mechs aboard."

"Maybe because you weren't supposed to know," Miles says, taking the gun away from the man in a clean, fluid motion. "And who the hell allowed you to bring this? We're in a pressurized tube traveling at subsonic speed. One shot would kill us all."

The man's face turns red, eyes narrowing on Miles. "I have a goddamn right to have it, that's why."

Miles pulls the clip and tosses it in a pod behind him. Still watching the man, he seals the pod. "Not on a sonic sub, you don't. And not with this team." He faces the other two, both women. "I suggest, if either of you are carrying, hand them over now."

The women glance at each other and show Miles they aren't carrying any weapons or guns.

"Good," Miles says and returns his attention to the man. "Report to your assigned duties."

The man's face still beet red, he storms away. He gives Ig a glare on his way by. The two women head for the door Ig almost opened earlier while Verity, Bracken, Miles, and Ash move closer to Ig in her mech.

"Well, then. I guess Leon managed to upload the tutorial," Bracken says.

"Yeah," Ig says, not sure if he can hear her or not.

Apparently, he does. "Good. We will be slowing down soon." He checks his watch. "In six minutes, actually. You will—"

The alarm sounds again, loud, even in the mech. The alarm cuts off, replaced by Leon's voice. "Murdock's subs are closing in. They've marked us."

"We need to slow down before reaching Mother," Bracken says.

"Can we go stealth in this thing?" Miles asks.

Bracken snaps his fingers and claps Miles on the shoulder. "We can. Good call. Leon, switch to full stealth and descend one hundred meters."

"At our speed, we can't—"

"Wait four minutes." Bracken dashes to the nearest seat and motions for the others to do the same. They all sit and strap in. "Has to be timed just right. At one hundred knots, go full stealth and descend at the same time."

"You better be right," Leon says, then adds, "Going full stealth in one minute. Hold tight."

"Thanks, Leon," Bracken says. She doesn't reply. He looks at Ig. "The mech has stabilizers. It'll take a hefty earthquake to kick it off its feet. Just hold still."

"Okay," she says, "but what about that guy? Isn't he—?"

"That guy has a name," the man grumbles as he storms by and takes a seat. "Ben."

"Ben Connally." Bracken taps his harness. "Buckle in."

Ben waves a hand. "What the hell do you think I was doin', man?" He buckles up.

"Ben here, is in charge of supplies, support, and weapons." Miles doesn't even look at the man when he speaks. "He's all we have in here to protect us from whatever is out there. Comforting, eh?"

"Fuck off, kid." Ben cocks a thumb at Miles, cold gaze on Ig. "Says the guy who killed most of his crew."

"That wasn't his fault," Bracken says, "and you know it."

"Yeah, well—"

All the lights shut off, dousing everyone in complete darkness. A few seconds later, mellow red lights along the ceiling blink on, slathering the sub in scarlet.

"Preparing to slow and dive," Leon says. "In three, two, one."

Ig doesn't feel any of it, but watches the others lift and slam in their harness. Heads bobble. Under any other circumstances, it might've been comical, watching them. Instead, it's kind of unnerving. They way they're whipped around, even in the harnesses.

It all lasts less than two minutes.

The lights remain red, however. Must be because of stealth mode.

Ben unbuckles from the harness, manages two steps, and drops to his knees. A gout of vomit splashes the floor.

"Christ," Miles growls.

"Where are the cleaning supplies?" Verity asks.

"If we have any," Bracken says, moving to Ben's side, "they'd be in the back. Should at least be a bucket and mop with some cleaner."

"Okay," Verity says and bustles away. She favors Ig with the sweetest smile as she passes and those dove wings in Ig flutter again.

At a near whisper, Leon's voice filters through the speakers in the sub. "We lost them for now. Whispers from here on out."

"We can talk normal," Bracken says. "I made sure sound-proof lining was added to every inch of the sub. Nothing above normal talk, though."

"Thanks for letting me know, jackass," Leon spouts. "Anyway, we are twenty minutes to Mother."

Bracken nods as he takes the mop and bucket from Verity. The bucket sloshes with cleanser. He mops up the vomit while Miles helps Ben to his feet.

"When she's in sight, slow us to a stop. We'll need to ascend at least forty meters so Ig doesn't have so far to go to collect the samples."

"Yes, your Majesty."

Bracken snorts. "Love you, Leon."

"Shut up."

Once Ben is escorted away by Miles, Bracken gestures for Verity to stand in front of Ig. Ash is tapping away on a tablet, pretty much ignoring everyone.

"Verity, Miles, and I will be joining you out there. Our mechs will be one of my older designs. We're to inject her with explosives after you take the samples. I can't stress this enough, though. Once you have samples from the lower torso, heart, and brain, get back here as fast as you can because it won't take us long to inject the explosives. Once we're aboard, we sonic-burst away and detonate. Crew after us will clean things up and take care of Murdock's guys."

Ig nods, though she hates every bit of this. She's supposed to be dumped in the open ocean in this thing? What if malfunctions? And what if—?

Bracken and Verity are knocked off their feet. A thunderous boom fills the mech. And, for the first time, she actually sways a bit. The stabilizers take hold, though, and the mech rights itself.

Before long, Bracken and Verity are on their feet. Bracken is shouting to Leon about a status report. Verity blinks, glancing around, as though waking up from a dream.

Miles stumbles around Ig and tells Bracken we've been hit. "Murdock's men found us."

Leon's voice is very frantic. "It's not Murdock's men. It's…it's something else."

"What just attacked us?" Bracken asks, making sure Miles is okay.

"Receiving input now," Leon responds.

Ash, placing the tablet in an open pod, helps Bracken place Miles in a seat.

"Ben alright?" Bracken asks.

"The bastard is fine," Miles says. "Shoved me away and got ahold of some straps so he wouldn't go flying. Me? I feel like a fuckin' pinball."

"Just sit still for a while," Bracken says.

"Duh," Miles says, more than a hint of frustration behind it.

A low, but annoying screech fills the sub, filtering in through the mech's speakers. "Looks like we were attacked by one of her offspring."

"Any details?" Bracken asks.

"Appears to be a crossbreed of *Mosasaurus* and *Liopleurodon*. Very large. Might be one of her guards."

"We just disturbed the hive," Miles mutters. "They're gonna protect their queen now."

Bracken glances at Ig and, in this instant, he seems defeated. Like this is it. Better to turn back now. Only lasts for a second, maybe two. Bracken straightens, expression hardening. "Get us within fifty meters of Mother. Ig is about to be deployed."

This jumpstarts her heart. No. She's not ready for this. She can't...

"And what are those two girls doing behind the door?" Verity asks.

"That's the bridge," Bracken says. "They're engineers."

"So, they control things here?"

"More or less. Leon has the final word, but yes, they do the real steering."

Verity frowns. "I don't get how you have things set up here. If they are engineers, why not let them control the sub?"

"They do," Bracken says. "They control every movement."

"So," Verity says, "why is Leon so involved? It's like she's controlling the sub."

"Why does it matter?" Miles interjects. "Leon is, by all accounts, our boss."

"Okay, look," Bracken says. "Leon is our guide. She oversees everything, but those two on the bridge, Emma and Brit, they decide what will be the best maneuver. Leon can't see everything."

"Says you," Leon whispers through the speakers.

Bracken mocks a heavy sigh. "Fiiine." He waggles his fingers like a mysterious sorcerer. "She knows everything."

"Don't be a smartass," Leon quips.

Bracken deflates. "Okay. Whatever. The point is, Leon sees all, but our engineers do the real work."

"I swear," Leon says, "you must've been asleep during our briefing."

A briefing that happened before Ig's group came through, she's sure. This is the first she'd ever heard of the briefing.

"I control the engineers, or rather, I give them the orders to do this or that. They can critique at their own will, of course, but I give the orders. I thought we went over this at one point?"

Bracken chuckles. "Just messing with you, jeez."

"So am I, jackass. Now, get Ignia into position for deployment."

Bracken salutes the camera. "Aye, Captain."

"And don't you forget it."

He laughs, shakes his head, and tells Ig to follow him. Before she turns away, she gives Verity a final glance. The woman is smiling. Ig smiles back, hoping Verity can see it. Then she follows Bracken toward the rear hull of the sub.

"I think Leon likes you," Ig says after a moment.

Walking beside her, Bracken snorts. "Shush, she'll hear you."

"Seriously. She's playing the tough-playful game."

He shoots a look at her, craning his neck to do so. "That's just weird. She's more like my sister. And I don't need another close relationship." He faces straight ahead. "Less hurt that way."

Ig opens her mouth, not sure what to say, but to at least say something—

Bracken flies off his feet, crashes into a set of wooden crates strapped to the floor of the hull. He grabs onto one of the straps, wraps his arm in. His teeth grit while he's tossed about like a cloth doll. Several booms and bangs crash through the mech's speakers. An eerie squeal snakes through the noise.

Just as sudden as it happened, Bracken drops to his knees, arm still wrapped in the strap above his lowered head. His chest heaves. A string of blood leaks from either his mouth or nose, Ig can't tell.

Through the speakers of the mech, Leon says, "We were attacked by a livyatan, crushed our flank pretty good, but so far we're not taking in water. Another big hit like that and the mission is a failure. Ignia, I need you out there. Be careful. The mech is built with weapons. Laser bursts and mini-torpedoes if you get into a jam but try not to use them. I can't see that far down the hull, is Bracken okay?"

Ig stares at Bracken. "He's not moving. There's blood."

"Shit," Leon says. "Okay, sit tight. I'll send Ash down."

"What about Miles and Verity?"

"They'll be seeing to Ben and adding support to our defenses until they need to be deployed too."

"Okay."

It doesn't take long for Ash to come sprinting into view. He skids to a stop and checks Bracken's pulse. He nods, mostly to himself, and gently unwarps Bracken's arm from the straps. Ash lays Bracken down on his back and checks the man's breathing. Again, Ash nods. He snaps a glance at Ig. "Tell Leon Bracken might have a concussion, but he will be fine. Just taking a bit of a nap."

Ig relays the message.

It takes Leon a full two minutes to respond. "Good. Have Ash get you to the deployment area. We're closing in on Mother. Time to lock and load."

Ig draws in a slow breath and blows it out slowly. She coughs, and is glad as hell Bracken was wrong about not being able to use the inhaler in the mech. She takes a couple puffs and tells Ash what Leon said.

He makes sure Bracken is in a spot where, if another attack happens, it won't hurt him anymore.

Ash faces Ig. "Let's go. Got to hurry."

He rushes on ahead, while Ig tells her mech to walk faster. She doesn't want to. In fact, she wants to tell Leon to shove it and get back to land. She has a mother of her own to take care of and precious little time to do it.

How the hell is she supposed to collect samples if there's a damn hive-like mentality out there? They'll tear her apart. And this, "Mother," what is she like? What kind of hell waits for her, writhing and biting in the dark fathoms?

Although, the monster isn't so deep, according to Bracken and everyone. Mother is maybe eight hundred feet down yet seems to float partially to the surface from time to time. Which is how she's being seen by satellites.

Maybe not dark fathoms, but there's darkness out there. Oh, yes. Darkness and madness, and Ig can almost feel the cold of the water. Can feel the pressure as some massive sea monster clamps her in its jaws and crushes her to death. Shivers scuttle through her.

"I'm staying on the sub," Ash says, "but will be in direct contact. I've been linking my tablet to the mech. I'll be able to show you the anatomy of Mother and where you need to draw the samples. Educated guesses, judging by the satellite images, but should get you what is needed."

Ig doesn't say anything. She's turning all this over in her mind. Trying to get a grasp on it. She's not a pro. She's never dived. She's never had to face monsters head-on.

She thinks about the old ways of her tribe. How every living thing is sacred and must be treated with respect. You kill a deer, you also drink its blood and give thanks to the winds and forest for providing you food. If you pick an apple, you give thanks to the earth. And so on.

What would her long-dead elders say now, knowing she's with a team who intend on killing a living creature?

What would her mom think?

They come to a large, round spot in the wall of the sub. Not far from this is what appears to be a clear pad of some kind.

"You have one minute to enter the deployment chamber before you're deployed," Ash says. "Sucks, but I can't control any of that from here. All I can do is seal the chamber after you're inside." He steps to the clear panel in the wall and—

"Wait," Ig says, edging toward a shout.

He frowns at her.

"I...I don't know if I can do this."

Ash, who she pegged as the nerd of the group, shrugs. The gesture isn't like something someone like him really does. He's supposed to be like a scientist. Critical, decisive, analytical, and factual. Dash in some experimental and there you have it.

And yet, this simple shrug strips that stereotype away. It makes Ash seem more human.

His left hand absently caresses his right wrist, where pink scars mar the flesh. "And maybe you can't. But we have to try. *You* have to try. This is bigger than simply destroying a monster. We'll save many lives with those samples. I fully believe that."

"Okay," Ig says, "but I've never done this before. I've never even dove as deep as ten feet."

He faces her fully then, hand falling away from the wrist. "The mech will do most of it for you. Like the ones we had in Lake Superior, it will filter the water through intakes and produce endless oxygen so you can breathe."

"Right, but I mean actually trying to take these samples. If her offspring are acting like a hive of bees and protecting their queen, how am I supposed to get close enough?"

Ash smiles. "That's where Ben comes in. He'll be spotting and stopping potential threats."

"Can we really trust him?"

He chuckles. "I hope so. But once Bracken, Miles, and Verity deploy, I'll be with Ben. Mainly to make sure he doesn't go berserk."

Ben has a good hundred pounds on Ash and taller by at least nine inches. Ash might be able to take the man on through intelligence alone, though. Brutes are brutes. Impulsive and strong. But a brute can be outsmarted. And if a person is quick enough, a brute can be easily dispatched.

Ig notes such strength in Ash's eyes. He can hold his own, if need be.

"Look," Ash says. "Don't worry. We all have your back here. We're all watching and making sure you're as safe as possible. Once you're about halfway through, Bracken, Miles, and Verity will be deployed to stop her." He glances around. "I'm not supposed to tell you this, but if they fail, we're to warp out of here to the mainland."

"We're just supposed to leave them out there?"

"There's another team, remember? They'll pick our people up."

Ig stares at him, at a loss for words.

"Ig," Ash says, voice gentle. "This will save your mother."

She draws in a breath, blows it out, and says, "Okay. Open it."

A smile lifts his face and she can almost see the ghost of before Murdock Jones got to him. "Be as quick as you can but have all your sensors and cameras on. It's three-hundred and sixty-degree security for eight hundred yards. You got this." He places his hand on the panel and a hole opens in the side of the sub to a small room. "The floor will open, letting you out. Let's save your mom."

She steps into the small room and the door whispers shut before she can change her mind.

"Well, that was stupid," she says to herself.

"Ignia? Did you say something?" Leon asks.

"No. Sorry."

"Prepare for deployment in: 3, 2, 1—"

"Wai—"

Even in the mech, there's a sense of vertigo. Where the solid floor ends, and one is suddenly falling. Even though you're not really falling.

There's a moment of utter claustrophobia while the ocean swallows her. A space in time where it simply can't be real. An almost euphoric rapture. Of—

"Ignia? You there? You are sinking fast. Need to turn on stabilizing thrusters." A pause. "Ig, can you hear me?"

She shakes her head, wheezing, and manages a quick pull from her inhaler. It's a tight fit, but at least she can manage.

Pocketing the inhaler, she says, "What do I say?"

"Did the tutorial not provide that information?"

"I...don't think so. Maybe, but—"

"Never mind. Say: Stability thrusts."

"Stability thrusts."

Even though she can't feel her decent much, the full-stop jars her. She jolts from the small seat, nearly cracking her head on the hatch above. Her teeth click together, somehow not slicing the tip of her tongue off. Stomach lurching, she fights down a surge of hot vomit.

It takes her a good minute for her body to equalize.

"Good," Leon says. "Turn on three-hundred and sixty-degree sensors and cameras. Mother will appear in the direction you need to go. She'll be, of course, the largest lifeform."

A headache pounds at her temples, but she remembers from the tutorial the command for the feature. At least she hopes it's right.

"Three-sixty surround monitoring."

A series of beeps and clicks fill the mech. All the monitors flicker on. Every one of them reveal something large, though none close enough to trigger an alarm. In monitor eight is a massive, red blob. Bigger than all the others.

Mother.

"Left side, minor burst thrust," she says, remembering the tutorial. The mech runs, though not quite facing the Mother's direction. "Left side, minor thrust." This brings her dead-on.

"Ig, Bracken here. You'll have to go full forward thrust to avoid becoming a meal to her offspring. The speed is over two hundred knots and should get you to her within a minute."

"How do I slow down before I get to her?" Ig asks. "I don't remember that in the tutorial."

"Right. Okay. So, you tell the mech to slow to medium thrust, wait a second or two, and tell it to go into low thrust. You don't want to go full stop, or you'll become a scrambled egg in there and the mech might buckle from pressure."

"Hey, thanks," Ig says. "I feel so much better now."

He snorts. "Sarcasm noted. Just ease into the stop and you'll be fine."

"How's your head?"

"Hurts like hell."

"I bet."

"Anyway, when you get to her, the places to extract samples from will be highlighted on monitor twelve. Follow it and move as quickly as you can. We don't know how she'll react, so…be very careful."

"Well, that sounds fun."

"I so miss that spontaneous sarcasm," Verity chimes in through the speakers. Ig smiles at the very sound of her voice.

"Hey," Ig says.

"Hey. You okay?"

"Oh…fantastic. Just floating here in the fathoms surrounded by sea monsters."

Verity giggles. "Just come back safe, okay?"

"I'll try." And she will. Because she must. For Mom.

"Remember," Bracken says. "You get close to her, gradually slow down. I'd say within thirty seconds."

"Okay."

She glares at the Mother of Monsters. This giant red blob like a cancerous growth. Killing it goes against everything she believes in, but it's something that must be done. Maybe the seas will once more be safe again. Although, she's heard of the Millennium Trench farther south where once prehistoric creatures are emerging. Some even mutated or accidentally spliced with other monsters, though none of the mythical nature, as far as Ig remembers from the news.

She focuses on the monitor showing Mother.

It's time.

"Full forward thrust."

In less than a second, she's hurtling through the water. A red counter in front of her reads: 30 knots.

Then: 80 knots.

Then: 200 knots.

She flies through the sea, everything a blur. Ahead waits only darkness. At least through the nano-glass of the hatch, anyway. On the monitor, the red blob fills the entire screen. In white letters and numbers at the bottom are: 36 secs till contact.

"Medium slow," she says.

The change is significant, though not entirely jarring. She counts to three, and says, "Low slow." Again, there's a moderate shift, slight shudder, and...

"Oh gods." She gapes at the monstrosity partially highlighted in the glare of her mech lamps. She's so caught up in awe she forgets something.

"Ig," Bracken says. "Stop!"

She blinks, shakes her head, and manages, "Stop."

The mech slows to full stop and before her is something out of even most imaginative writer's nightmare. A great thing that should not be. A being beyond sanity. She knew Mother would be big, but this...this is mountainous. A true titan of the deep.

She can't even tell where the creature begins or ends. Mouths, some with teeth, some not, snap and chomp at the very water itself. Maybe they're eating plankton? She can't tell for sure. The mouths cover most of what she can see of its bulbous body. Hundreds of them. The body itself resembles a pot of pea soup dashed with fish scales. Light green and gross looking.

A huge great white shark darts into view, nudges the creature, and veers toward Ig. It surges forward, and she braces for impact. The shark's mouth snaps inches from the mech, then it's yanked backward in a storm of scarlet.

When the blood finally clears, she gapes in horror while two of the mouths rip the great white apart. These mouths, they have lips. Almost like humans. They suck the flesh right off as jagged teeth pulverize the bones.

The shark is gone in less than a minute.

"Ig," Bracken says. "You need to move. Now."

Her nerves spark, jerking her out of the horror show. She glances at monitor twelve. According to this thing, one of the spots, the abdomen, is directly in front of her. She lifts her head as black tongues lash out, snatching chunks of shark meat from the water. Her stomach churns.

"Ig, you need to—"

"I know! Shut up and let me think."

Lovely silence floats through the mech. She returns her attention to Mother. At all those thick-lipped mouths writhing in a stew of scaly green flesh.

"Needle," she says, remembering the tutorial commands.

A muffled hum follows a sharp click and a needle as long as she is tall shoots out like a knight's lance from the right arm of the mech. She gapes at the thing. No one told her she'd be jousting.

Yet, in a way, perhaps that's exactly what she's about to do.

"Prepare for sample extraction."

Whirring fills the inside of the mech for a couple seconds. "Sample extraction online." Monotone, robotic. Very mech.

She readies herself for full forward thrust. Time to get this over wi—

A sharp whistle breaks her concentration. Red light flickers on her right. Heart thrashing, she glances at the left flank monitor. There are two set side by side. One reveals the distance of the danger, the other shows her what it looks like and possible species.

400 yards.

Megalodon.

"You fucking kidding me?"

"You have one shot at this," Bracken says.

"That's reassuring."

"When it reaches fifty feet, shut off stabilizers. You should drop out of its path before it gets to you. Its momentum will carry it far enough away for you to take the first sample and move on to the next extraction point."

"*Should* drop?"

"If the mech doesn't sink fast enough, trigger the dive thrusters. Be quick, though. Don't hesitate too long. She's comin' in fast."

"You know," Ig says, "you never said anything about any of this, right? On the beach or in the bunker, or wherever the hell that was back there."

"Well, I needed you."

"So, you, what? Lied?"

"Bent the truth. Pay attention to—"

"I did the training, but never during all that time did you once say this bitch's offspring would be protecting it like godsdamn bees!"

"I did say you might be in a mech, though…"

"Ugh. Yes. Okay. You mentioned it. But it was all offhanded and shit. You need to—"

"Enough," Leon shouts, severing the mild argument. "Ignia, that megalodon is now one hundred feet. You need to listen to what Bracken says now. And Bracken...*really*? You never told her fully what she might be getting herself into?"

"Okay," Ig says.

"Well, I got her to join up, didn't I? We needed her."

"I swear to God, I'm gonna slap the shit outta you later," Leon says. "Ignia, sorry about all this, but you need to shit of the stabilizers right...now."

The monitor flashes bright red.

"Stabilizers off!"

The sensation is almost dreamlike. Falling through cotton. There's a sense of vertigo, though nothing jarring. It's a gradual thing. It's...

Going much too slow.

The gaping, toothy cavern of the megalodon is about twenty feet away, but it might as well be inches.

"Dive thrust!"

She's shoved downward at gods knew what speed. Fast enough to change the scene in front of her from all teeth to utter darkness in less than a blink. Deeper into the black stew of the Devil's Trench.

"Stabilize," Bracken says. "She swept past. Get the sample and move to the next extraction point."

"Stabilize thrusts," Ig says. The mech slows to a stop.

Above, she sees only darkness. The only danger is Mother straight ahead in her great, red, blob taking up the entire monitor.

Images of her mother, frail and in bed. Her mother unable to go to the bathroom on her own. Her mother battling a patient beast.

Ig's gaze narrows. Her heart thuds like a wrecking ball in her chest.

She positions herself using small thrusts, aiming upward a few degrees.

"Don't go at her at full speed," Bracken says.

A grin cuts across her face. "See you on the flipside, Brack."

"What? Ig—"

"Full forward thrust!"

The darkness gives way to the green, scaly flesh littered with snapping mouths and her grin never falters.

CHAPTER 12

The gray is like a thick, rippling soup. Peaceful. Empty, yes, but the silence is beautiful here, bobbing and listing. A buoy untethered drifting in a vast, gray, nothing. His own, secret ocean.

He could float in this soup for eternity and never wish for more. Because this is it. This is better than money. This is greater than power. This is…oblivion. His way out of the madness.

He's thinking he might just let himself sink into the gray soup when the ripples around him tremble. Small waves lap at him like swollen dog tongues. Dead dog tongues. Shivers rack him as the warm soup turns cold. He thrashes, confused. What—?

The small waves, they say, "Mr. Jones? Sir?" Over and over and over. This voice in the waves. Waves growing bolder. Waves becoming whitecaps, churning and tossing him around. He flails, trying to find something to hold onto, but, of course, there's nothing. He's in the soup. Once warm, loving, and calm; now vicious, cold, and utter turmoil.

"Mr. Jones? Sir, I need you to wake up."

He screams just before a large, rolling wave crashes over him. Tumbling in the cold gray, he holds his breath. He fights for the surface but every kick or lunge feels too slow. He's too tired. Maybe he should just breathe it in, the soup. Let it fill his lungs. Maybe that's what he's wanted to do for a long time. Let it end. Perhaps his daughter is waiting for him. Perhaps—

"Mr. Jones." The voice is much louder. So loud now, it *is* the soup. A living, evil thing ready to consume him.

It's not his choice to surface. More like someone yanking him out.

He gasps, sputters, and—

"Mr. Jones. There's an urgent matter you need to attend to."

His eyelids flutter, life returning to him with all its pain. The vast sea of gray soup drains away and he's left shivering on a cold, stone floor.

No one bothered to put him in his bed.

Bastards.

"Mr.—"

Eyes opening, he grips the throat of the young man hovering over him. The young man clasps both hands over his. Murdock sits, throttling the boy. All his hate and rage shoots down his arm to his hand.

He clutches tighter, drawing the young man's choking face close, he says, "Who the fuck are you?"

The boy glugs and spits. His face is turning a deeper shade of red.

Murdock growls, shoves the young man away, and staggers to his feet. The floor shifts and rolls like a waterbed for a moment or two. He keeps his balance by holding onto the edge of his desk. The man, sputtering, whining like a beat dog, crawls away.

"I don't know you," Murdock shouts, glaring at the boy. "Do you have clearance?"

The young man, coughing now, gains his feet and stumbles toward the door.

He doesn't look back before he leaves.

Breathing heavily, Murdock slams a fist down on his desk. He's not sure why he's so upset, nor why he wanted to kill that boy. And he would have too. He would've strangled the boy or crushed the windpipe. Whichever happened first.

But, he let go. Not because he wanted to, just...he's not a murderer. He's not—

The phone on his desk beeps, signaling an incoming call.

A shuddery breath escapes him, too haggard and loud to be a sigh. He shuffles to the phone. He wishes nothing more than to smash the godforsaken thing. Instead, he taps the answer icon on the display.

"What?"

"Mr. Jones, there are matters which require your immediate attention."

The buzz of alcohol fades enough for him to think. "What is wrong, Captain Sullivan?"

"We lost a team. There are more creatures than the large one and they appear to be defending her like..."

Murdock plops into his desk chair, head throbbing and missing the gray soup of his dreams. "Like what, Captain? Spit it out."

"I don't know, like ants defending their queen, I guess. One of the creatures bit Team One's sub in half. Team Two has fallen back and awaits further orders."

"What of Mr. Tull's team?"

"We know they're there, we just can't see them. Their cloaking is much too advanced for our sensors. Though one has been deployed, from what we can tell. A mech, if our high-density cameras are correct."

Tweezing the bridge of his nose with his thumb and index finger, Murdock sighs. "Of course, it's a mech. Mr. Tull is obsessed with the damned things. Can we get a lock on the mech and seize it?"

"All attempts have failed, sir. Range too far. The situation is dire, losing Team One. Would it be wise to continue pursuing Mr. Tull's team, or remain out of danger until we have a clear way?"

"And what way would that be?"

"When their team needs to flee, they will need to drop their cloak for an instant. It will be enough to lock on and capture their vessel. This way we don't compromise the lives of Team Two."

Murdock's hand lowers from his face and leans forward, glowering at the phone display. "Those are not my orders."

"Sir, I—"

"Who was the young man who entered my chamber?"

Sullivan falls quiet for a few seconds. "That would be your new assistant, sir. Michael Davis."

"Next time wait until I'm awake to send someone. I about killed him."

"Noted, sir."

"Goddamn better be. Now, I want Team Two to get in there and seize the mech. I don't care about the sub."

"Sir?"

"Mark my words, it's that mech that's collecting samples. They're trying to steal from me and I want them in custody."

"How will we know they've collected enough?"

"Lay low," Murdock says. "Near the bottom and monitor. If the mech succeeds, it will haul ass to Mr. Tull's sub. Catch it before that happens." He leans back in the chair, hating the fogginess of his head and how his guts twist like mating snakes.

Sullivan takes a while to respond, long enough for Murdock to nod off a bit.

"And if Team Two is discovered, sir?"

Murdock wakes with a snort. "Huh?"

"If Team Two is discovered, what then?"

"Well, shit, Sullivan, our subs have signal deflectors, right? Turn those bastards on and keep them on." He tries to keep himself from losing his temper too much, but these days…

"And if they have counter detection?"

Murdock shoots out of his chair, rage burning a new hole through his very soul. He picks the phone up and roars at it. "I picked you fuckers for a reason! Do your goddamn job!" With another roar, he throws the phone across the room. It crashes into the aquarium with the dead frill shark, shattering.

Heaving breath after breath, he collapses into his chair.

A few seconds later…he's swimming in the gray soup again.

CHAPTER 13

She stabs the needle deep into Mother, somehow managing to avoid the snapping mouths and lashing, black tongues.

"Commencing plasma withdraw," the robotic voice of the mech announces.

To her left, a mouth as large as a small car snaps and grinds its teeth no more than six meters away. On the right, a black tongue snaps like a whip, falling several inches short of her.

"Come on, come on," she says through gritted teeth.

"Fifty percent complete," the mech announces.

"Extraction will take a minute at each spot," Bracken says.

"Hey," Ig says. "Thanks for the heads up."

"Sorry. There was a lot happening all at once and this little detail escaped me. You're in a good spot to avoid those mouths, and Mother must not feel the needle, otherwise she'd be attacking in some way."

"Well, isn't that just lovely."

Giggles. "You better make it back here alive," Verity says. "Because I want to kiss that sarcastic mouth of yours."

Ig smiles. "I—"

"Extraction complete," the mech interrupts. Because it's a machine, apparently it has a right to be rude.

"Thanks, mech," Ig says. "And Verity…see you soon."

Verity doesn't say anything more.

Ig yanks the needle out of Mother's massive abdomen and pushes herself away a few yards. She checks the monitor telling her where to go next. The chest. The heart. A good two hundred feet above. What other horrors await her up there? A mild shiver scuttles over her skin. She hates to think about it.

And maybe that's the key. Not thinking.

She read somewhere if a person thinks too much during a time of crisis, they'll end up dead.

Perhaps this is true here too.

Directly above her is a mouth. This one, though, appears not to have teeth and sucks at the water rather than snap at it. A creature as massive as Mother, she must need all the food she can get, which probably includes plankton and whatever else those sucking mouths capture.

She waits for Bracken to give her some words of wisdom, but he's oddly silent right now. Maybe she should ask him what to do? No, she knows what needs to be done. She doesn't need him to hold her hand now.

Ig draws in a breath, positions herself upward, and says, "Full upward thrust."

She's not sure it'll work at first, then—

Before she has time to really think, the mech slams through the puckering, toothless mouth, leaving its weird lips in tatters, and hurtles upward.

"One hundred feet to destination," the mech says.

She tells the mech to swerve when needed and all is going well until something huge and dark shoots out of a crater-like pore and, like a damn windshield wiper, swipes her mech away.

The world becomes a twirling, flipping mess, even while the stabilizers try to correct the hit. She tumbles and everything outside the mech is silvery bubbles and darkness. The motion forces her stomach to churn and she struggles against the vomit boiling in her throat. There is no up and down or any sense of direction.

All is madness.

The mech chirps and beeps until the thing finally stabilizes itself. Her head whips to the side when all is said and done. The beeping stops and the mech tells her it is acquiring equilibrium and to stand by.

Still, no word from Bracken or anyone. Never has she felt so alone. The mech is a tomb. She'll die in this dark trench. Maybe Murdock Jones found them. Maybe he killed them all. The mech filters water and creates air, but for how long? Or, rather, how long will it last until she reaches shore? And that's if she isn't eaten by some monstrosity from the deep.

"Equilibrium achieved," the mech says. "Relocating target."

Her heart stammers. It remembers what she was doing? It—

Without any commands, the mech readjusts itself and shoots toward Mother. Ig has no control over this and she braces herself for whatever lay ahead.

As the mech draws closer, never letting up speed, she's convinced it's committing suicide. Either that or one of Murdock's cronies tapped into its programming and is going to end it once and for all.

"Mild thrust," she manages through a tightening chest and cramping throat.

Thankfully, the mech slows a bit.

Ig, wasting no time, brings out the inhaler and takes a couple puffs. She stows it back in her pocket, sighing in relief, and blinks at how close she is to Mother.

"Slow thrust," she cries.

The mech jolts, slowing to a crawl about ten meters from Mother and the ravenous mouths. She's not far from the chest area, according to the monitor.

"What happened?" Bracken asks.

"What…happened? Really? You didn't see it?"

"I was kind of indisposed. Had to break away for a while to deal with something else. I thought you were heading for the heart minutes ago."

"Uh, I was, until a tentacle shot out of a pore or whatever and smacked me away. I'm about to that point now."

"Pore? Hold on. Stabilize until I can gather some info quick."

She sighs. "Hey, sure. The Mother of Monsters and I are just gonna kinda hang out here."

Bracken doesn't respond.

"Stabilize," she says.

And here she floats in a space between the mouths and wherever the pore with the tentacle is. Here she waits, though itching to get moving. Ready to end this. The sooner she can collect the samples, the sooner they can get back and hopefully develop a cure for Mom. That's what matters right now. All that matters. This is for Mom. But, maybe, it's also for Ig. Maybe a small part of her is loving this. The action of it. The terror in knowing that at any moment something might—

The sensors bleep once before giant jaws clamp down over her. Caught between pointy teeth, the mech tries to stabilize while whatever has her swims off. In the monitors, she catches a fleeting glimpse of Mother, then…darkness. Alarms beep. A pressure warning winks on monitor one.

She struggles in the heavy jaws. The top half of her is inside the mouth while her lower half dangles outside. The teeth have her pinked in the middle. She jabs the needle at a thick tongue covered in bristles. Blood wells, but the jaws don't let up.

"Ig? What's going on?"

"The hell does it look like?" she shouts. "Something got me. I don't know where it's taking me."

"Laser burst," Bracken says. "Left arm of the mech, fire a laser burst into the back of its throat, if you can."

Brain frazzled, she shakes her head, trying to remember the command for the laser burst. For a few godless seconds, she can't remember anything. Then…it all clicks together. She shifts a bit, positions the mech, and lifts the left arm.

"Laser."

A bright blue beam shoots out, followed by a blaze of red. The burst strikes the back of a shiny throat.

Everything quakes. Even through the mech she feels it. A loud shriek somehow filters through the speakers. And then...

She's free. Tumbling into the cold, dark fathoms of the Devil's Trench, the mech sputters.

"Stabilize."

The mech continues sputtering and she continues sinking into the inky black. How deep is the Devil's Trench? How much pressure can the mech take before buckling?

"Stabilize!"

Nothing. All the lights flicker. The monitors sputter. A shrill whine fills the mech.

Static, littered with bits and pieces of Bracken's voice. Though, no matter how much she tries to tell him what's going on, he either can't hear or can't understand what he's trying to tell her.

"Stabilize, you piece of shit!"

Down and down and down, tumbling into complete darkness. The mech's lamps flicker, hardly penetrating the absolute black.

She holds her breath, waiting for the depths to claim her.

Giving up, she awaits her watery tomb.

CHAPTER 14

When he wakes, he's alone. As he's always alone, but at least there's not some boy here trying to shake him awake.

Sullivan should've known better.

Murdock stretches in the chair, back crackling like cellophane. Pain laces through his lower back and neck. Aches plague both knees.

He hates getting old. No matter how rich a person is, and with all the remedies to slow aging, time catches up with everyone. Aging is eventual. Perhaps the creature out there will have an answer to stop aging, perhaps not. He needs to see. It's his last hope. To bring back his beautiful daughter and stop him from aging, at least until Anna is fully grown.

Murdock stands, waits for his balance to return to him, and walks to the tank. The other fish have nearly picked the frill shark clean. Nothing but bones and a few fins left. On the floor is the shattered phone he vaguely remembers throwing.

Need to calm down on the drinking, he thinks as he makes his way across the room to the kitchen. Food. Yes. He needs something to soak up the remnants of alcohol and get his brain back in working order again. In the fridge are a dozen bottles of water, meats and cheeses, and various other contents he needs to explore. Rarely does he need to make his own meals or snacks, but it does happen from time to time when he grows weary of being catered upon.

He's not helpless, after all.

With a grunt, he hauls out all the meats and cheeses. Sandwich meats, mostly, though there is a nice container of brisket brought in from just the other day. It's this he heaps onto a bread slice, places a couple strips of cheese on top and crushed a second slice of bread on top. He's ripping into the sandwich when a slow knock echoes through the chamber.

He swallows. "For fuck sake. Can't I get a few hours of privacy?"

The knocking continues.

"Jesus Christ," he bellows. "Come in already!"

From the kitchen, he has a clear viewpoint to the door. He takes another bite out of his sandwich, watching the door open. It's not the young man who enters this time, but Captain Sullivan. The man, no older than forty, hurries to Murdock's desk. He stops at the tank with the skeletal remains of the frill shark and picks up the broken phone. He stands, glances back and forth. Utterly lost. Still carrying the broken phone, Sullivan rushes toward the back of the room where Murdock's bedroom rests.

Murdock grins, lazily finishing his sandwich. With the weight of food in his stomach, his mind finally finds itself. He finds a bag of potato chips and opens them.

Sullivan is still in the bedroom.

What the hell is the guy doing, anyway? One glance would tell him Murdock isn't there. What's he doing? Sniffing underwear, or something?

Finally, Sullivan emerges. Even from where Murdock stands, munching on his potato chips, the man's face is one of bewilderment and fearful concern. What's passing through Sullivan's mind right now, Murdock wonders. Is the man thinking, perhaps, that Murdock has killed himself and is lying somewhere hidden? Or maybe he's thinking Murdock just up and ran off? Possible. Ah, but he's not as mad as everyone thinks he is.

Not while there's work to be done.

Murdock, finishing the last of the chips, crumples the bag up, making as much noise as possible.

Sullivan nearly jumps out of his polished boots. He spins, almost stumbles, and spots Murdock.

"Mr. Jones?"

Murdock chuckles and tosses the empty chip bag in the trash can. "Well, it's definitely not Jesus Christ. What do I owe the honor, Captain?"

Sullivan, at first, appears leery, hesitant. As though Murdock is a ghost or something. Finally, however, he breaks free of this and strides over to the kitchen.

"Team Two was discovered and attacked."

Murdock nods, smiling, and grabs himself a bottle of water from the fridge. He twists the cap and guzzles down almost half the bottle.

"They had to evacuate to a lower depth in the trench. Damage is minimal. Appears Mr. Tull's crew only shot partial laser bursts. Nothing strong enough to do much damage."

Murdock leans against the counter. "Warning shots. Mr. Tull is nothing if not courteous, eh? Get our team out of those depths. Did they lock onto Mr. Tull's vessel?"

Sullivan sighs. "No. They didn't have time."

"Fair enough. Get the team out of the trench and hang back one hundred meters. They'll know we're there, but if we don't attack, they won't worry about us too much. It's not them we want…it's that mech."

Sullivan visibly gulps, glances away.

"What?"

The captain straightens a bit. "Well, sir, some hybrid between a mosasaur and possible megalodon got it. We lost visual and presume the mech and person inside is dead."

Murdock rocks off the counter and snatches Sullivan by the collar of his uniform. "You telling me we lost the one thing we were banking on?"

The captain's gaze fixes on Murdock. A respectable trait, looking a man in the eye like that. "It appears so. We're not certain, though."

Murdock releases Sullivan and grips the man's shoulders. Not hard, but firm enough to drive home who's running the show here. "Good thing we have our own little ace up our sleeve, right, Captain?"

When Sullivan appears confused, Murdock throws back his head and barks laughter at the ceiling. It's a fit he hasn't had for a very long time. Laughing, truly laughing, hasn't been a thing since Anna was still with him.

He gives Sullivan a shove and spreads his arms out. "You think I'd tell anyone about my backup plan? Hell, for all I know you're working with the Resistance, Captain Sullivan."

"M-Me? Sir, I—"

"Oh, shut up, man. Listen here, there is a secret operative with Team Two. My backup in case bullshit like this happens. Be prepared, that's the motto, right? Damn right. So, all I need to do is send the signal and he'll suit up and deploy immediately. If we can't get Mr. Tull's crew to get our samples, then, by God, we'll get it ourselves."

Sullivan frowns at Murdock for a second or two, then straightens himself. "Am I to know the name of this man, so I may aid in surveillance to protect him, or is he on his own?"

"You will be linked, yes." Murdock waves a hand. "Go back to Command and watch my boy do what he does best."

The captain begins to turn away, stops. "Sir?"

Murdock lifts an eyebrow in question.

"When was the last time you had a psych eval?"

"What the hell kind of question is that, Captain?"

Sullivan shakes his head. "I mean, you've been under a lot stress lately. You used to be—"

"Captain Sullivan," Murdock says. "If you wish to walk out of my chamber, I suggest you shut your goddamn mouth and follow orders."

The captain blinks, nods, and bustles away.

When the door closes behind him, Murdock finishes off his bottled water and walks to the tank. He picks up Anna's skull, tears prickling his eyes. Cradled in the crook of his arm, he makes his way to the bedroom.

It isn't much, the bedroom. Small, with a bed, TV, and emergency phone. There's also a spacious bathroom connected. The bed...he can't remember the last time he slept in it.

It's not the bed which draws him here, though. He steps across the room to the small bar. A good knock of scotch has always helped him sleep well. His fingers brush the second blue tile in from the wall to the far right. He taps the tile and steps back.

A mellow hiss. The bar slides aside and from the floor a glass tube arises. The tube, it's about two feet wide by a good four feet long. Inside this tube isn't water, but an electrized clear fluid. Floating in this fluid is a brain, eyeballs, and the entire nervous system of the human body.

Wiping tears from his cheeks, lower lip quivering, Murdock places a trembling hand on the glass.

"Anna," he manages through a whisper, and lowers his head.

In the tube, the brain and eyeballs bob. Neither appear to notice his presence.

CHAPTER 15

"Online. Online. Online."

Ig blinks, glances at the monitors. All the lights stop flickering. The monitors are solid and—

"Ig! Can you hear me! Ig, please respond!"

"Hey," she says, as the mech's lamps sputter on.

"Thank Christ," Bracken says. "Thought we lost you there."

"Mech went weird. Wouldn't stabilize."

"It took some damage and needed to make a report. It's fine, though. Damage was nothing but scratches and gouges in the metal."

"Well, isn't that fantastic. How far away from Mother am I?"

"About one mile. Don't turbo boost back; that will only drain the mech's energy. It replenishes, but it's better you have marginal rather than a little when you get back here."

"Lovely. Well, see ya later."

She takes a deep breath, blows it out slowly, then positions herself upward. "Full forward thrust."

Ig shoots out of the darkness and into thick gray. Like soup. About the same depth as Mother's chest, she assumes. Well, above the abdomen, at any rate. She shifts her direction and flies through the water. If there are any monsters nearby, the sensors don't spot them. Then again, the sensors didn't see a threat until it was too late earlier.

She put too much trust in technology and nearly got eaten because of it.

So, she keeps her sight peeled for anything, as well as watching the camera monitors for any more movement. Still not promising. If something is going to attack, it will do so just as fast as last time. Maybe one of them will finally be the can opener to end it all.

This, she hopes, won't happen. Though it's true. They're protecting their mother. And what good child wouldn't protect their mother? She doesn't blame them for that. Just wishes they'd understand what she's trying to do.

Or maybe they do, in some primal way. Maybe they get it and are trying to stop it. Humans, after all, have ruined Earth. Humans alone, and no one wants to own it. Not one. If one is not of the Earth, like Ig's tribe, one will never understand the tortures humanity creates. Eventually, the planet is going to give up trying and simply die. She's not so sure she wants to be around when that happens. It's sad to even think about.

Before long, the sallow green scales of Mother comes into view, like an ominous beacon.

She aims herself upward a degree.

So far, there aren't any dangers being sensed, nor monitored. She doesn't see anything with her own eyes either.

Needle still extended, Ig powers closer to Mother. Now, the mouths come into view. Soon enough, she surveys hundreds of pores or craters littering Mother's bosom. Every so often, a black tentacle whips out for no apparent reason at all. Fat breasts float up and outward and…

"What the hell is sucking on them?" she asks herself.

Dark tentacles wrap around each breast. The bodies are elongated, huge and pulsing, like black pustules about to burst. The creatures are just about the size of the massive breasts they suckle on.

"Move on," Bracken says. "Heart will be between the breasts."

The spot isn't far above. A few feet, give or take. "Slow forward thrust." She's within striking distance now. "Stop. Slow upward thrust."

"There you go," Bracken says. "Nice and easy. Soon as you collect the sample, get out of there and full thrust upward. The closer you get to her head, from what I'm seeing, the more offspring you'll encounter."

"Well, doesn't that just sound grand," Ig spouts. She thinks Bracken chuckles, though she's not sure.

She's getting used to this more sarcastic side of her. Embracing it, even.

Growing up, she never had very many friends. Those who were moved away once they got old enough. None of them were from her tribe. The tribe Murdock Jones saw fit to annihilate.

Thinking about it heats her blood. If she even comes face to face with that monster…

She's about to pass the spot between breasts and calls for the mech to stop. The sensors remain quiet. All the monitors are clear, well, save for Mother directly in front of her and the things suckling on her breasts.

Ig draws the mech's arm with the needle back, sucks in a breath, and plunges the needle through the scales and into the heart. At least that's what the imagining across the mech's glass reads.

"Begin sample extraction," she says.

"Beginning sample extraction," the mech responds and a dull whir drifts to her ears.

"We're monitoring your perimeter," Miles says. "If I have a shot, nothing will touch you."

"Where were you before?"

He grunts. "Ben and I had a minor disagreement. It's taken care of now."

"Oh, gods, you didn't kill him, did you?"

Faint chuckling. "No. He's right here. My wingman. Say hello, Ben."

"Hey, Ig."

She smiles. "Hi, Ben. Better behave now, huh?"

"It's not that," Ben says. "I—"

"He forgot who outranks him is all," Miles interjects. "Happens to the best of us. No hard feeling either."

"Agreed," Ben says. "No hard feelings."

Ig blinks. "Who are you and what have you done to Ben the Asshole?"

This garners laughter from everyone listening, by the sound.

Look at you, she thinks. *A godsdamn comedian in the making.*

"Sample extraction at 50 percent," the mech announces.

Ig opens her mouth to ask if Verity is around to chat when Mother does something she hasn't done since they've been here.

Mother moves.

It's more than a shift. All the green scales flap, smacking at the needle still inserted into her heart. Ig maneuvers the mech as best she can, praying the needle doesn't break.

ALS is a neurological disorder. What's the central point of every nervous system? The brain. She needs the fluids of Mother's brain most of all. Not that she knows this, exactly, but it makes sense.

"Whoa," Bracken says. "Hold tight, Ig. I don't know what she's doing yet."

"Holding," Ig says between giving the mech commands and—

"Aw, shit," Miles bellows. "Shit just hit the fan. Don't move, Ig."

"Huh? What? What just hit the fan?"

From Miles or anyone, there are no answers. She glances at the monitors, though all they reveal is the thick, gray soup of the ocean. Then all her sensors go off at once. In monitor two, she catches a glimpse of something dark. Monitor five appears to writhe with snakes or worms. But this can't be possible because…

"Holy shit," Bracken says. "They're krakens."

"I got it," Miles says. "Just a little to the—*there!*"

A strong force shoves the mech into Mother's bosom. As a result, the needle plunges deeper.

"Sample extraction at eighty percent," the mech tells her.

Something thumps against the mech's nanoglass hatch. Then something else. This is followed by more thuds and clunks. She glances around, finding the water filled with debris. The tip of a dark brown tentacle twitches as it floats by in front of her.

"Got it," Miles says. "Ben's locking onto the second one."

"You—you're telling me those are real krakens?"

"Yep," Bracken says. "Far too large and mean to be giant squids."

"Not full grown, though," Leon says, speaking for the first time in what feels like forever to Ig. "These are babies."

"Babies or not," Ben says. "They're pissed and protecting their mom."

As a good child should, Ig thinks and sighs.

Parents start out as the protectors, but by the end, it's the children who must take care of and protect the parents. It's just the circle of a thing called life. Round and round we all go. Over and over. That's just how it is. As it should be.

She can't blame the monster's babies for trying to protect their mother, but if the oceans and all life are to return to some resemblance of normal, this mother needs to be stopped. As sad as it is. And as much as Ig is against it, this Mother must be destroyed. Ig hates the idea of killing a creature who only wishes to survive like everything else on the planet. She blames her culture and beliefs, and those don't make her wrong.

Right or wrong. Who is to say which is what?

"Sample extraction complete."

Ig pulls the needle free. Still, bits and pieces of the kraken Miles blew up floats and swirls. As though, even in death, the baby knows who its mother is and refuses to leave. Nature, even in monsters, has its primal affections and links to emotions only previously found in humanity. Do monsters fear? Yes. Do monsters love?

Yes.

"Full upward thrust, Ig," Bracken says. "Miles, Verity, and I will be deploying soon to place the explosives."

She still can't accept the fact. Mother needs to die, and yet…why? It comes to her soon enough, though. Accepting breeds understanding. Mother produces far too many offspring per hour to be sustained. They'll eat the food of other marine life, then the marine life and so on. They'll be like a plague through the oceans. Consuming and leaving nothing but death in their wakes. It has already begun…

Was it Leon or Bracken who said almost the same thing not so long ago?

Ig can't remember, but surely one of them said so. If not, maybe she truly has fallen off the nut-wagon in Crazytown.

"Ig?" Bracken says, sounding a bit irritated.

She shakes her head. "Full upward thrust."

The mech complies. She shoots upward, past the bosom. Where the second kraken is, she doesn't know. Hopefully Ben has changed his tune; otherwise, a mythological monster might very well be stalking her.

The speed of the mech slicing through the water is so intense, she can't get a grasp on it. It's fast enough to disorientate her just enough. Ig lolls in her seat, somewhere between consciousness and vomiting. Her gaze drops away from the monitors. For what feels like forever, she lists inside the mech, though it's no longer than two minutes.

Through the glaze of nausea, Ig glimpses a huge, dark, soulless eye. "S-Stop."

Not going through the slowdown procedure, a full-stop slams first her butt into the seat then the top of her head into the glass hatch. She utters a groan, rubbing the top of her head.

Once the pain in her head fades and she's seeing clearly, Ig gapes at Mother's head. Or rather, three dragon-like heads on thick, serpentine necks. The one closest appears to yawn. A titan's jaws weary of the small things scattered about. A proverbial god unimpressed.

Mother doesn't even appear to notice Ig. Regardless of how close the mech floats, the enormous creature glares on without qualm. If those obsidian eyes are watching her, she can't tell.

"No one told me there'd be three heads," Ig says.

But all she gets in response is an earful of static.

A frown wrinkles her face. "Bracken?"

No answer.

"Miles?"

Nothing.

"Leon?"

More static.

Tears prickling her eyes. "Verity? Anybody? Hello?"

The static cuts off, filling the inside of the mech with silence. Stark and utter silence. The emptiness of a tomb is this quiet.

"Hel—"

"Iiiigniaa…" a soft whisper slithers through the speakers. Or is it in her head?

"Wh-Who…?"

"Iiiigniaa…"

She glances around, checking every monitor, and that's when she sees it. Not far off, something that resembles a mosasaur, only with dozens of long, black tentacles like a massive kraken. It doesn't attack, but instead floats about on fifty meters from her back. Its vulpine head lowers, and she understands. It can take her out any time it wants to. A greater power is keeping it from doing so.

"Iiiigniaaa," the whisper fills her head. Yes. It's in her head. Not through the speakers. It's really a voice in her head.

Is this how madness starts? Confusion? Voices? The eventual mutterings of old gods and a lunatic's grin?

Ig shudders at the thought.

"You have taken from me, Ignia."

She refuses to respond. Because if she accepts the thing, then the thing will be real. She can't let insanity win. She must fight. She—

"You are not going mad, child. This is me speaking to you."

"Who?" It's all she can manage, hating herself for giving in so easily.

"The one you keep taking from." While the words are spoken, all three dragon-like heads swivel in her direction.

Ig gasps.

"Yesss..."

Ig shakes her head. "You're not...you can't be..."

"But I am, child. And you are meddling." The voice pauses, as though in reflection. "I have always been, child, and I shall always be. The thing that should not be risen from this ancient trench where I've been buried for far too long."

"M-Mother?"

"Is that what you call me?" A pause. "Perhaps it is all that makes sense to you, though not what I am. Still, yes, call me Mother if you wish."

Ig's gaze lowers to the mosasaur creature. It hasn't moved. Its head is still lowered like a wolf about to take down its prey. On the other monitors, other creatures appear. A giant shark, no doubt a megalodon. The shifty kraken itself. And what appears to be a massive sea serpent.

She blinks and gasps when the ocean, the mech, everything is replaced with tall grasses swaying in a mild summer breeze. Above, a bright sun bakes warmth into the land. She opens her mouth—

"You think Iowa is as beautiful as Oregon?"

And when she turns, Ig realizes she's lying in the grasses beside someone. Someone she knows very well. But it can't be...

"Ig? Are you okay?"

Her body snuggles against Ig's. A familiar warmth Ig has all but forgotten, until now.

"Anna?"

The girl smiles up at her. Just as much warmth in that smile as the slender body along Ig's But, this can't be right. Can't be real. Even so, the grass under her is just as soft as she remembers. The scent of nearby pine trees, the green of the tall grasses, and the gentle lavender of Anna's perfume dance in the perfect summer air. Swirling and dipping and swirling. A beautiful waltz. Ig can't help but be taken in by it all.

"I'm going to miss you," Anna says and Ig's heart melts.

This has happened before. Yes. Six years ago, if one is counting. So, Anna can't really be here because—

"But I *am* here, baby," Anna says, voice like a purring kitten in Ig's ear.

How did she...?

"Know?" Anna giggles and gods, it's been so long since Ig has heard such sweetness. "Because we can be together again, Iggy. We can have the life we always talked about. I won't move away this time. I promise."

Ig, despite everything, smiles. Oh, how she's missed her love. To actually be lying in these grasses with the heat of the Oregon sun (something that rarely happened until after the climate shifts) with Anna is something she's missed greatly. Love is love. And she loved Anna. Or is it loves now?

Has everything up until now just been a sickening nightmare?

"Yes," Anna says. "You were asleep and crying. More like a daymare, though." She giggles in her incredibly cute way again and strokes Ig's arm with her slender hand. "All better now."

"My mom?"

"What about her? She's picking sweetcorn at the house, baby."

Yes. Mom said she was going to pick corn that day. Or today? What the hell is even going on? She can't pinpoint any of it and, really, why should she? Maybe it had all been a dream, as dark as they come. Maybe she's been given a second chance.

Ig cups Anna's cheek. "Don't go."

Anna frowns. "You know I have to. My dad—"

"Shut up," Ig spouts, hating the harshness in her voice, but unable to control it. If this truly is a second chance, then she needs to put a stop to what might happen. "Your dad will have to deal. Stay with me. Going to Iowa is a mistake."

Anna snorts. "You don't know my dad. Besides, I'll be fine. Two years, tops, and I'll be right back here." She gives Ig the brightest smile. "With you."

"A lot can happen in two years," Ig says, heart sinking. Hasn't she spoken those words before? Maybe...

"Hun," Anna says. "Dad is paying for this. When I get back, I'll have a job in his company and we'll be living the dream." She keeps her lovely smile. "Promise."

Ig shakes her head, moving away from Anna. "No. That's not how it'll happen if you go."

"How do you know?"

"Because you get sick and die before you even board the plane."

To this, Anna gapes at Ig. She doesn't move for at least a full minute. Finally, Anna says, "How do you know that? Seriously, you're freaking me out."

"Because," Ig says, mulling the answer over. "My nightmare. I don't know. All I know is you need to stay right here. With me. Don't go."

Anna's face contorts. She shoves away from Ig. For the first time since dating Anna, Ig sees the girl's father. That rotten bit of the Jones gene. It's there, then gone as Anna gets dressed.

"Look," Ig says, also standing. "It's not that hard. Just stay with me. Don't let him control your life."

Anna spins on her, face a specter of fury. "My dad will not allow it. Why can't you see that? He'll pry us a part, just so he gets his way. I'm his only child and heir to his business. I *have* to go."

Ig doesn't get it. Not then, not now. She grabs Anna's arm, trying to think of anything that will make her change her mind and coming up short. Just as she had before. Or she *has*…something. Her mind is so muddled with clashing realities, she doesn't even know what's left or right, up or down. She doesn't know if she's still alive or not.

Ig yanks Anna to her and places a fierce kiss on the girl's lips. The taste is just as divine as she remembers.

When they part, Anna blinks, their gazes link.

"Y-You really want me to stay?" Anna asks.

"Yes. Stay here with me and we'll make a good life. We don't need your dad."

Anna appears to think this over, then smiles. "Okay." She snuggles into Ig's arms. "I love you."

Ig kisses the top of Anna's head, breathing her lavender scent. A smile warms her face. This. This is all she's ever wanted.

Could it all have really been a dream? Maybe Anna really didn't leave. Maybe this is the true reality? Maybe…

"No," the voice of Mother whispers. "This is a dream, Ignia. This is what was lost, though could be once more. Life is a wheel constantly turning. I can bring this moment back for you, Ignia. I can make everything right."

"What about Murdock Jones?"

"In this timeline, he will suffer a major heart attack, leaving everything to Anna. Anna will not be sent to college in Iowa. She will not fall ill and die. Your mother will not be dying."

Ig kisses the top of Anna's head again. "That's all I want. She's all I want." Then she frowns. "Wait, what about my mom?"

"Ignia...come now. Do you not realize Murdock Jones was responsible for injecting your mother with ALS parasites? Aggressive ones at that."

"What? Why?"

"Because he wanted vengeance. He blamed you for Anna's illness, so he wanted to take someone you also loved in return for his. Surely you know this."

Ig shakes her head, tightening her hold on Anna. "No. I mean, I suspected, but—"

"ALS has been determined to be a parasite that eats away at the brain and nervous system. Murdock Jones extracted a particularly rare form of the parasite from a thawed corpse one his teams found in the northern tundra. An old sample he found to get back at you."

She has nothing but a nod. She doesn't want to believe it, but it makes sense too. Mom's ALS flared up out of nowhere. Not even a warning. One week she was fine, the next, her hands were gradually losing strength. Another week, and those hands lost a lot of their muscle, becoming skeletal hooks. Hands which simply refused to function no matter how much Mom tried. From there...she just got worse. Mom is a fighter, but the disease, those damned parasites, were eating her alive.

And now...

What about now, in this reality?

"Murdock dies," says Mother. "Anna lives. No one injects your mother with the parasites. Anna gains her father's business and she sells it to the Government. You all live full, wealthy lives." Mother sighs. "Now, isn't this the reality worth pursuing?"

Ig still clutches Anna. "Yes." Tears squiggle down her cheeks. "It's all I want. Her and Mom. My family..."

"I can give this to you, child." A pause. "All I ask is for you to stop. You don't float far from me. Stop this nonsense. Stop taking from me to give to others when what you give will not save your mother, nor will it bring Anna back. My blood will not cure anyone."

"How?" Ig manages. "How will you give this reality to me?"

There's a pause. Long enough for reason to set in.

Ig gasps. "You're lying."

"I never lie, child."

"You..." Ig glances at Anna and holds her away at arms-length. There is not enough air in her lungs to scream.

Anna is nothing more than a skeleton patched with black mold. Her clothes hang on her like tattered rags, mouth yawning open in a silent scream.

Ig releases the shoulders and steps back.

"Ig?" Anna's voice float from the skeleton's mouth. "What's wrong, baby?"

This isn't real, Ig tells herself. This isn't—

"It can be," Mother whispers. "All you have to do is...stop..."

"Really?"

"Yesss..."

Ig stares at Anna's skeleton.

"I can't wait to be with you forever," the skeleton says in Anna's voice.

And, gods help her, Ig almost accepts this reality. Almost concedes to Mother's will. For, yes, this is the perfect life. One with both Anna and Mom still alive and healthy. A life without worry or hurt. Just a happy life. Don't good people deserve good lives?

But...but...but...

No.

"I can't," Ig manages, shaking her head.

The skeleton in front of her screams. It lurches forward, bony hands grasping. Ig slaps the hands away and shouts, *"You're not Anna!"*

Those cold, bony hands scuttle around her neck and...

Blink.

Ig stares at Mother. Only the nearest head is looking at her now. "The choice is yours, child. Yield and let me give you all you ever wanted or die. You and all your friends. What would your mother think when you never come home? What, I wonder, will be her final thoughts about the daughter who abandoned her as she lay dying?"

Images of Anna's bright, smiling face flickers before her mind's eye. Ig chokes down a sob.

Can it be? Really? Can she have Anna back? Can she save Mom from—?

Static crackles through the speakers, severing her thoughts. Severing...the illusion. The static grows and within this noise comes a voice. A very familiar one.

"Ig...don't...on our way!"

"V...Verity?" Ig shakes her head, vision swimming like she's had a few too many drinks.

"Laser bust," Bracken shouts through the static.

This smacks whatever dizzy sensation she has in her out. She coughs, sucks in a breath, and suddenly everything is crystal clear.

Mother glowers, very close to Ig. Close enough to open those jaws and swallow Ig whole. "There is no hope here, child."

With a cry, Ig stabs the entire length of the needle into Mother's eye. "Begin sample extraction!"

"Beginning sample extraction, now," the mech says.

Mother doesn't move, nor does she speak for the longest time. The speakers are still full of static and all her monitors have gone black. She doesn't care. What matters is getting the samples to the sub and hauling ass out of here before all those offspring are given the go-ahead to kill. But...

"Sample extraction at twenty percent."

It's taking too long. Soon, whatever that mosasaur thing was doing will snatch her up and eat crush her like a soda can. Or maybe a something else from Mother's ovaries will—

A bright blue flash to the right draws her attention. Just in time to see massive jaws filled with foot-long teeth snap shut inches from her. A shiny blue mech, much more formfitting than hers, slams down on the monster's back and slices its head off with a laser. The head rolls away from the body, bobs and thumps into Ig's mech before floating out of sight. Bubbles blow out of the ragged stump of neck as the body sinks, black tentacles writhing.

It was the mosasaur creature. The—

"Goddamn Leviathan," Bracken shouts through the static.

"Sample extraction at seventy percent."

"C'mon," Ig says. "Hurry up."

"We are too many," Mother croons. "You shall not make it out of these waters alive."

"Sample extraction at eighty percent."

"This world will be ours, child." The other heads of Mother swivel in Ig's direction, both revealing long teeth in their dragon-like jaws. "This is the end."

The second head snaps out at Ig, missing her by mere centimeters. Heart bashing itself against her ribs, she commands the mech backward two feet, hoping like hell it doesn't affect the extraction.

The third head snakes around the second, stretching its length. Its giant maw opens. This is it. It has her. All because the stupid, godsdamn extract—

"Extraction complete."

Ig yanks the needle out of Mother's eyes and manages, "Full right thrust!"

Her body slams into the left of the mech. It surges sideways in a curtain of bubbles and torn flesh. A roar fills the speakers (or is it in her head?) quaking all her resolve and sending her asthma into overdrive.

Iron bands clamp around her chest and throat. The more she tries to ignore them, the tighter they get. Cinching and crushing. She struggles, fighting the attack with sheer will. It's something she tries to do with every attack, unless her mind is elsewhere. Build the will up. Grow stronger. Maybe not need to use the inhaler so much. Exercises in will. Unfortunately, some illnesses can't be exercised as much as others. Asthma being one of them.

She draws the inhaler from her pocket, finally relenting, and sucks in puff. She waits, and inhales another. The iron bands gradually lift. Ig sighs with relief while the mech continues slicing through the water sideways. She doesn't want it to stop. For all she cares, it can travel all the way to the mainland. Bracken, Verity…they can take care of themselves.

"Slow thrust," Ig says. And when the speed is right, she shouts, "Full stop."

The mech stops, whipping her around inside and yanking on the harnesses holding her relatively in place. Once equilibrium catches up, Ig gapes at the darkness. She's not sure how far she's gone.

She makes sure all sensors are working. They are. But there's no sign of the sub. All the monitors reveal nothing but the bleakness of the Devil's Trench.

"Bracken?"

Nothing. Not even static.

Shit, maybe she powered out of range? Ig is about to turn around and head back toward Mother, when Leon says, "I'll uncloak for fifteen seconds. Reach us by then or wait for Bracken and the others to return. You have one shot right now. Make it count."

Before Ig can even gather her bearings, the sub slickers into existence not far to her left. Maybe forty meters. She doesn't consult the sensors, aiming herself toward the sub.

"Full—"

Before she can say the command, a black net snaps over the mech. She goes about cutting the net with the laser, but…

"This is USS *Snare*," a hollow voice filters through her speakers. "Comply and be taken aboard or face serious consequences."

"Fuck off," Ig says, and cuts through the net using the laser. "Full forward thrust." She speeds through the water to her sub.

It doesn't take long to find the spot where she was deployed.

"What's going on, Ig?" Miles asks.

"USS *Snare* just threw a net on me. Almost to the deployment spot. Someone letting me in?"

"On it. Ben is trying to locate those bastards right now."

"Well, that's comforting. Ten seconds."

"Ignia," Leon says. "You'll lose visual in the sub in less than ten."

Before the woman has time to finish, the sub winks out of existence.

"Full stop," Ig shouts, taking the brunt of the sudden jolt. She slams forward in her harness, thanking whatever gods there are that the mech has a harness. It hurts like hell but could be much worse.

"I'm tracking you," Miles says. "Follow my directions and you should be good."

"Okay."

"Slow forward thrust."

Ig nods. "Slow forward thrust." The mech whirs and floats forward.

"You're about twenty feet from the deployment area, Ig."

"Fantastic. You sure I can't go medium speed? I feel like an elderly woman in a Wal-Mart scooter."

Faint chuckling. Miles says, "That's probably the best analogy I've heard for a mech speed. Anyway, easy does it. You're now nine feet away. Straight course."

"Gotcha. I—"

Another black net snaps over the mech, crisscrossing the nanoglass of the hatch. She's about to use the laser to cut through it like the last one when a dull thump echoes through the mech.

"Shit. They shot an EMP onto—"

A loud whump and everything in the mech goes black. The lights cut off. The gentle sigh of the mech producing breathable air wheezes to silence.

"No," Ig says. She taps the monitors, punches at buttons. She shouts for help. All to no avail.

A slight tugging sensation and all she can hear is the shuddering of her breathing. How long does she have before running out of air? Can't be long, especially with how frantic her lungs are working, as though she's already running out of air. Maybe because she is. Any moment now, it'll become a fight for every breath. And when she runs out of air? What then?

Then...you die, a grotesque voice whispers in her head, strikingly similar to Mother's voice.

She draws in a couple puffs from her inhaler and waits. Maybe the mech will come back online.

Loud clunking and the mech turns. She gapes at the gray, slatted bottom of a sub. This one much larger than Bracken and Leon's. The belly of the sub opens up, shining bright light into her face. She's dragged into this light, this belly of another beast. For, there is no doubt in her mind, USS *Snare* is Murdock Jones's doing.

The man who sent her beloved Anna away and didn't even try to save his only child. The man who, if Mother is to be believed, injected

Mom with ancient parasites that gave her an aggressive form of ALS. There is no other word for Ig's feeling for the man as hate. Pure hate.

But, what if Mother was lying? Quite possible, since the monster obviously wanted to send Ig into madness.

Madness...

For all she knows, she's fallen off the nut wagon in Crazytown long before this. What sane person would accept such a mission, anyway?

Ig's breathing becomes more labored as she's lifted into the belly of sub.

Running out of air, she thinks, hand stealing instinctively for the inhaler in her pocket again.

Without the stabilizers, the mech falls onto its side when she's lifted, and all the water drains away. She glances around, but the nanoglass fogs over before she can see anything. Through the mech, she hears nothing. With it offline, she's both deaf and blind. Her heart trip-hammers. Shivers of ice cut through her. What does Murdock's crew want with her? She's a nobody. Why not Bracken or Miles?

A sharp, metallic clink followed by a massive whoosh. The hatch lifts, exposing her to relatively fresh air and a dozen men with guns pointed at her. The man standing closest, a frown creases his chubby face.

He steps forward a bit more. "Who are you?"

Ig looks away, not complying. Her name won't mean anything, but damn it if she'll make it easy for them.

"Are you an officer?"

Once more, Ig keeps her gaze from reaching the chubby man.

"Speak!" Ah, now he's good and pissed off.

Ig looks at him. "Are *you* an officer?"

"Captain Jenkins of the US Navy Seals."

"No shit? How does an honorable Seal get tangled up with a monster like Murdock Jones?"

Jenkins gives her a withering look. "Just tell me your name and rank."

"No."

"It doesn't matter," a deeper voice says. She can't see who's talking. "She has what he wants. Let's go home."

Jenkins nods and steps away from her. "Prepare for rapid drive." He looks at Ig. "You'll be fine where you are. Just don't get out of the harness."

She doesn't say anything and hopes Bracken and the others will come after her.

There is never a guarantee in life.

Such as now…

CHAPTER 16

"We have the samples, sir," Sullivan says as he opens the door and steps through into the chamber. "An indigenous woman is in a mech with the samples."

Murdock was about to simply wave Sullivan off until the mention of "indigenous."

He frowns. "What is the name of this indigenous woman?"

Sullivan shrugs. "According to Admiral Kelly, she refuses to state her name and rank."

Murdock turns away from Sullivan, playing on a hunch. "I want this woman brought to me as soon as our team reaches sore."

"Very well, sir." Sullivan leaves the chamber, forgetting to close the door behind him.

Murdock paces. Could it be? After all this time…could it be her?

He stares at the frill shark skeleton floating on the surface of the tank.

Sometimes the skeletons in one's closet never truly get buried.

Murdock grins, striding toward the bedroom.

There's much to do.

CHAPTER 17

A shrill alarm sounds and if the mech was safe to breathe in, she might've shut the hatch. With everything shut down, all she can do is hope for the best. No way in hell is she going to get out of the mech, though. It's her lifeline, despite it being a worthless mountain of metal right now. At least it's something.

She lies on her right side in a large, round docking area of some kind. With no stabilizers, the mech lolls and clunks against the curved walls of the dock. The sub is in motion. It—

A small, red-light, blinks to the left of monitor one.

Heart tumbling over itself, she taps the blinking light. Miles's face flickers on the monitor.

"Ig," Miles says. "Bracken tapped into the sub-cell battery and comms boards of the mech. We don't have long. We're in pursuit, but we need you to reboot the mech while there's still some juice."

"What happened?"

"They attached a small, mobile EMP. It'll keep knocking out power until it's removed."

"How the hell do I remove it, then?"

"You have to get out and pry it off. The sub-battery will last for ten minutes after this transmission. Once you get the EMP off, buckle back into the mech and close the hatch. Once you reboot, everything will seal, and you can be ready for us."

"Wait, how do I reboot?"

"Manual toggle switch," Bracken says, somewhere near the camera. "Behind the head rest. Flip it up and down twice when the EMP device is removed."

"Okay, but—"

The monitor goes black. "Transmission ended," a small voice says. Nothing like the loud monotone of the mech, but similar enough.

"Shit," she says and unbuckles the harness. She peeks out of the mech.

The room she's in isn't huge, but much larger than anything in Bracken's sub. Everything is covered in shiny steel plating, mirroring her grimy face back at her everywhere she looks. Gods, she needs a shower.

Regardless, the room is empty. She crawls out of the mech and climbs to a grated floor. Water sloshes a foot or two under her boots.

Ten minutes. That's all she gets. And if she doesn't get everything done in ten minutes?

She doesn't even want to think about that right now. The sub is hurtling through the water at speeds unknown and she feels it. It takes her much longer than she wants it to, like slogging through knee-deep molasses, to make it around the mech. She spots the EMP device right away. Like the room, it's plated in shiny steel. She grips onto the thing, pulls. Doesn't budge. Some kind of magnetic force, maybe?

Ig climbs out of the docking area and stumbles around, searching for a pipe, or anything she can use to pry the damn device off. At first glance, her heart sinks. There's nothing but shiny metal everywhere. Hell, she can't even see where a door might be. She glares at herself everywhere she turns. How do the people working on this thing not lose their damn minds?

Just as she's about to give up, her gaze fixes on something. And she might not have seen it not for the slight curve in the wall. A corner? Ig makes her way across the room to a series of pipes protruding from the floor and disappearing into the ceiling and yes, it's a corner. With all the polished shine, it created a weird illusion of nothing. She didn't even see the pipes until now.

Optical illusion or not, the darker length of metal broke the spell. And here it is. She picks up a three-foot-long wrench. Heavy as all hell too. In a couple pipes, there are valves. No doubt the wrench is used to release pressure when needed. Whatever it's used for, she could care less.

Ig hurries as best she can back to the round dock area. She clambers down to the grated floor and swings the giant wrench as hard as she can. The EMP device peels away a bit with a metallic screech. She swings again and again until the device flies off, smacks into the far wall of the docking area, and crashes to the floor. Blue sparks spill from a gash left by the wrench.

She drops the wrench, trying to ignore the tightness in her chest, the swollen throat, and wheezing breaths, and climbs back into the mech. She buckles into the harness, shuts the latch, and feels around behind the headrest. There she soon finds the toggle switch Bracken was talking about and—

The world becomes a jumbled mess as the mech slams into a wall of the docking area and flipped around like a ragdoll. Ig, crying out in both pain and terror, flips the switch up and down once.

A loud hum fills the inside of the mech, followed by a long hiss.

Ig gropes for her inhaler, but the mech is once more knocked around and she has to try and block any possible head injuries. When everything calms down again, she manages to take a quick puff and shoves the inhaler back in her pocket.

All the lights in the mech sputter. The monitors flicker. She has a few hellish seconds when she doubts the mech will fully reboot and—

All the monitors go live. The hissing stops and she breathes in fresh air. A small whirring remains for another few seconds, then that too falls silent.

"…hear me?" Sounds like Verity.

"Hello? Yes, I hear you!"

"Ig." Verity's sweet voice. "Thank God. Was getting worried you wouldn't get the mech online in time."

"I got it, hun. Now what?"

"Just sit tight. Bracken and Miles are doing some heroic shit."

Ig snorts, not sure if Verity is serious or not. "What?"

"You're supposed to just stand by, beautiful."

This warms Ig's heart a bit. She's never thought of herself as beautiful before. At least, not after Anna died. And now…

"Will you…" Ig manages, "will you stay with me until they do whatever they're doing?"

The pause is so long, Ig is sure Verity never heard a word, but… "I will stay with you forever, if you wish."

Tears fill Ig's eyes. For the first time in a long time, she has finally found love again. Or, in the very least, found something close to love.

"Stabilizers online," the mech announces. "Do you wish to stabilize?"

"Yes," Ig says, though off-handedly. She's still thinking about Verity.

The mech rises, hatch sealing, Once the machine is upright…

"Stabilized. Do you wish to maneuver?"

This…she's not sure of. Maneuver to where? Then, an incredibly evil idea occurs to her. She could use the laser and cut a hole in the floor of the dock. She would be free, but…what of the people on the sub? Just because they follow Murdock Jones, does this mean they're evil too? Surely not all of them. She's been wrong before, though. For all she knows, every man on the sub is an utter asshole, rapist, murderer, and pure evil. She doesn't know them, nor will she ever have a chance to know them.

Still, they're human beings. They're lives she can't jeopardize.

There's only one option, then. She turns and faces a gleaming wall. A wall offset only by a small panel not far to the right. The panel has only two buttons: Red and green. She walks and mech walks with her. In fact, it doesn't feel as though she moves her legs, but she does. There's little to no resistance. Using her own movements, she makes the mech slam a large hand over the green button of the panel.

All the lights dim. A warbling siren wails through the mech's speakers.

"Ig," Verity says. "I was just told to tell you not to hit the release button in their deployment bay. You'll be—"

Then everything is a tumbling, bubble-filled mess.

She catches a sliver of a glimpse of doors slipping shut, extinguishing all light. Then it's all darkness and constant flipping into oblivion. In the oblivion, there is nothing but insanity. You tumble and spin and know for sure you're going to die. You just know you're going to slam into something and be crushed or broken, or in the very least, bruised to all hell.

There is no light and apparently the lamps on the mech haven't registered the change in ambiance because they haven't turned on yet. It's like being stuck in a Tilt-O-Whirl at a county fair in gods know where Iowa or Minnesota. The shifting back and forth, the spinning. The dips and surges upward. All of it happening at once, only stuck in a dark room. There's a sensation of motion but seeing this is impossible. Maybe she should feel lucky she can't see anything. Wouldn't be good to puke in the mech.

She screams at the mech to stabilize, but it must be hurtling through the water too fast to take hold. The word WARNING flashes across the nanoglass, but she's not sure what kind of warning it is. Like a pinball tilt warning, maybe? This is what it feels like, anyway. Like she's a pinball bouncing off bumpers and rolling in every direction. Maybe it is a tilt and the entire thing needs to be restarted?

Hopefully, this isn't the case, but it's a worry gnawing at her with every flip and tumble. It's all too much. She can't stop the screams blowing out of her.

She's still screaming when everything stops. A massive, jolting stop which finally breaks her. Ig barely gets a hand over her mouth before vomit spurts. Most of it bibs her front and pools in her lap. A reeking mess that, thankfully, didn't splatter the monitors.

A meaty burp bubbles out of her throat and she thinks she's about to puke again when Bracken says, "Gotcha. Just sit tight. Bringing you aboard."

Ig sways in her harness, drained and gagging on the stink. A noxious cloud she can't avoid or even hide from. Her eyelids slip shut and when she opens them again, someone is talking to her.

How long was she out?

Apparently not very long because she's still in the mech. A sliver of time stolen from her.

Blinking, Ig forces down hot bile crawling up her throat. The smell. It's too much.

"Ig?" Verity calls. "Are you okay in there? You're safe now."

Ig fears opening her mouth might give her body a signal to vomit again, but manages, "Puked."

A slight pause before Miles says, "I would've too. Open'er up and we'll take care of you."

"O...Open hatch," Ig whispers, head lolling, and slipping out of time again.

***

Murmuring voices float around her like the ghosts they are, though she refuses to open her eyes.

Not yet.

Her head feels like it's been filled with water and mud, and it's all just sloshing around in there.

The murmurs soon meld to echoey thrums and finally...words.

"...dead. All of them."

"He's gonna come after us now."

"Let him. Been waiting to take that fucker out for years."

"We can't go back to base now."

"Have to. Leon needs those samples and we made a promise to Ig."

She coughs, eyes opening to dull, blue light. Looking through a lens covered in a veil of gauze, this is what it's like. Ig rolls onto her side, shivering at the cold metal under her. Realization washes in soon enough.

She's on the floor of the sub. They must be cloaked, which explains the dim, blue light.

A warm hand touched her forehead. She flinches, sucks in a breath, turns, and—

"Shh," Verity says, face calm and beautiful in the pale blue glow. "It's just me. How are you feeling?"

When she opens her mouth, a dry wheeze floats out. She clears her throat, hating the taste of vomit still lingering on her tongue, and tries again. "Like shit."

"You took a hell of a tumble out that sub," Miles says, crouching beside Verity. He flashes a pen-light in her eyes, nods. "You'll be alright." He places a hand on her arm. "You kicked ass today." He smiles, straightens, and walks away.

"I got the mech cleaned out, hun," Verity says. "No worries."

As embarrassing as it is, Ig smiles. "Thank you." She tries to sit up, but gravity yanks her back down. "Wh-What's going on?"

"You blew their seal," Bracken says, kneeling. He takes up the spot where Miles had been. "Their sub exploded. No survivors."

She shudders out a weak breath. "Oh, my gods…"

"I know," Bracken says, lowering his head a bit. "No one is supposed to die. Especially like that. But, it was the only way we could get you back before they reached the mainland. Their sub was much faster than ours."

Ig gropes for her inhaler and Verity shakes it in front of her. "Here."

Verity places the mouthpiece in Ig's mouth just as Ig draws in a breath. Pshht. The medicine gradually relieves her wheezing.

"Thank you," Ig tell Verity.

The woman waves a hand at her and places the inhaler back in Ig's pocket. "I'll always be there for you."

A spark, hell, a flame, ignites in Ig, and she hopes Verity feels it too. The heat. The attraction…

If Verity's smile is any indication, yes, she feels it too.

"He's tracking us," Ash says, though remains out of view.

Bracken frowns. "How?"

"Not sure, yet. Maybe a bug somewhere, but—"

Bracken stands. "What?"

Verity helps Ig into a sitting position.

Ash glances up from his tablet, eyes wide. "I'm getting an incoming call."

Bracken and Miles exchange a glance.

Ash shoots a look from one to the other. "What should we do here?"

Bracken nods. "Answer it."

"Are you sure—?"

"Yes." Bracken takes the tablet from Ash and taps the screen.

A voice Ig only heard in vague passing a little over six years ago, echoes through the sub.

"Why, hello, Mr. Tull! Long time no see. How's the wife and kid? Dead? Oh…sorry to hear that. Looking a bit grizzled these days too."

Bracken, gripping the sides of the table so tight the plastic creaks, glowers at the screen. "Soon. Soon I'll kill you."

Light chuckling. "Is that so? Well, I welcome you here. All of you, in fact. But...especially little Ignia. You there, dear?"

Bracken shoots a frown at Ig, shakes his head. "She's sleeping. What do you want?"

"You are a horrible liar, Mr. Tull. Where is Ms. Hawkins? I wish to speak with her."

"Murdock—"

"I can send a satellite EMP to your sub right now, Mr. Tull, and kill you all. Do not tempt me. Let me speak with Ignia Hawkins and you all just might live to see the mainland."

Ash slinks away, though only Ig notices. She's about to say something when Bracken spouts, "Fine. Ig? The bastard wants to talk to you."

She tries to steel herself from his condescending tone and arrogant grin. But, no matter how much she tries, when Bracken turns the tablet, Ig's heart whip-cracks. Staring at your dead girlfriend's father does this, but also when you suspect the man of injecting your mom with parasites, giving her an advanced form of ALS. Less than a year ago, Mom began to decline.

And yet, what if the Mother of Monsters is wrong?

Murdock Jones does not grin, but smiles. Something bordering warm, though not quite. It's those steely eyes. They never change. There's no doubt in her mind she's staring at a serpent. One that appears docile enough until it strikes.

"Ms. Hawkins!" Murdock chuckles. "How have you been, dear?"

She doesn't reply; instead, Ig finds the strength to stand.

Murdock cocks his head to the side, as though in question. "Well now, that's no way to greet an old friend, is it? What would Anna say?"

"She'd say you're a heartless bastard." Ig finds her own strength as she takes a couple steps closer to the tablet. "She'd say you set her away, not because of the education, but because she was in love with another girl."

This pauses Murdock for a moment. Though, only a moment.

Now, finally, his shark's grin surfaces. "Ah, now…that's cutting a bit deep, isn't it? I loved my daughter."

Ig feels the bewildered gazes on her and ignores them. This is greater than all of them right now. "No, you didn't. All you were doing was grooming her to take over when you retire."

"I was giving her a secure life," Murdock blasts. "Everything I did, it was for her!"

"You fucking liar," Ig shouts. "You had her set to leave and whatever the hell you were meddling in at the time got her sick. Ancient spores is my guess."

He visibly winces at this, and she smiles. Eventually, he clears his throat and runs a comb through his black mustache. And, oh, how she wants to see a red, smoldering hole in his forehead right now.

"Ignia," Murdock says, "Ms. Hawkins. We both...loved my daughter. But it wasn't my fault, nor your own how she died. And this matter, right now, is beyond that."

"You injected my mom with ancient parasites!"

He opens his mouth, then closes it. For a good twenty seconds, the man says nothing. If she ever needed the truth...here it is. Ah, but he's also a snake and snakes are great at camouflage.

"I don't know what you're talking about, dear Ignia. I always liked that name, you know? Ignia. So beautiful. Rolls right off the tongue. I see why my Anna loved you...even if she didn't know what she was doing. You have a true, fiery spirit. I admire that in a person."

Diversion, persuasion...manipulation. Gaslighting at its finest. Only a monster is this cunning.

"Bullshit," Ig says. "You know *exactly* what I'm talking about. You blamed me for Anna getting sick, so you did what would hurt me most. You injected my mom with parasites and gave her a rare form of ALS."

"How do—?" He stops himself, but it's already too late. The guilt overshadows his pallid face. Murdock runs a hand over his slicked-back black hair. His face flushes a tad. But only a tad. After a couple seconds, he sighs. A chuckle rattles out of him. "Okay. I think you need to stop living in whatever fantasy land you've taken root in and listen to me. You will peacefully hand over the samples you took from that creature. You will do so alone. No Bracken. No whoever else is on that sub with you. You do this simple thing, and I will give you this..." He holds a thin vial filled with green liquid.

Ig frowns. "What the hell is that?"

A smile curls on Murdock's face. "Something I'm sure you have prayed for since your mother got sick." He gently shakes the vial. "A cure."

Her heart thuds. "What?"

"It's not a cure, Ig," Bracken says. "He's just trying to trick you into giving him what he wants."

"You were always a fool, Mr. Tull. That's why you never gained success with your mechs, you know. You are an utter fool."

"Fuck you." Bracken turns the tablet around so it faces him. "You prey on people. You use them to get what you want then get rid of them like kicking trash into the gutter. You're a worthless, hollow, piece of shit who knows his time is about to end."

Murdock's chuckle is dark and low. "Ah, Mr. Tull. You amuse me with your fervor. Put Ignia back on, please? I am not finished speaking with her."

Bracken sneers but turns the screen back to Ig.

Murdock gives her a wink. "There we are. Now…" He holds up the green vial again. "This is the cure to stop and reverse the ALS your poor mother suffers with. She will not be the same as she was before the disease, too much damage too quickly, my doctors say. But, she will be cured. This, I promise you, if, and only if, you deliver the samples to me personally."

At a loss for words, Ig can only gape at the vial of green liquid. Finally, she shakes her head. "And if I don't?"

He lowers the vial and his face contorts in mock sorrow. "Well, my dear Ignia…" He steps out of frame, and she stares at her mom lying in bed. On the floor is the caretaker Bracken sent to help. No matter how much she tries, Ig can't think of the woman's name. It's right there on the tip of her brain, and yet…nothing. She hates that she can't remember the woman's name.

Mom isn't tied to the bed and there's a short man in a white lab coat standing on the opposite side of the bed from the woman on the floor, sweeping some black object back and forth.

"As you can see," Murdock says, still out of frame. "We came to pay your poor mother a visit. Don't worry, she is fine. Well, as fine as she can be in her condition, of course."

"You bastard," Ig shouts. "What the hell are you—?"

"Don't worry, Ignia. If you deliver the samples in five hours, your mother will live for you to give her the cure. If you're not here in five hours, however…" He once more steps out of frame.

The small man with the white lab coat places a scalpel on Mom's throat. Mom's eyes are shut, chest slowly rising and falling. They drugged her, no doubt.

Rage spills through Ig. "I swear to all the gods that ever were, if you hurt her—"

"You are not going to worry about that, Ignia. What you *need* to worry about is being here in five hours. Less, if possible." He steps in front of the camera again, obstructing her view of Mom and the short man with the scalpel. He sighs. "This is not how I wanted this to go. If you had just let my people bring you home…all this could have been avoided."

Ig wipes away stray tears, hating how weak they make her appear. "What did Anna die of? Really. Don't bullshit me."

He glances away for a moment, and when he looks at the camera again, there's genuine pain in his eyes. A slight shimmer of tears. The first true emotion she's seen from him so far.

"Unknown illness," he says, voice choked. "Even my doctors and scientists couldn't figure it out." He fetches a heavy sigh. "That's why I need those samples. For her."

"What do the samples have to do with Anna?"

He opens his mouth, then thinks better of it and shuts it again. The pain in his eyes vanishes. Just like that. Poof. Gone. "Five hours, Ms. Hawkins. Don't be late. I—"

A tiny beep, and she gapes at the home screen of Ash's tablet.

"How the fuck did he tap into us?" Bracken shouts. Either at everyone or himself, Ig isn't sure. Nor does she much care.

Her mind storms with thoughts. So many she can't pin them down. She stands, a woman at a crossroads, lost. There is no right or wrong. No up and down. She's here, and yet not…

"Ig helped in the tap," Ash says, hurrying into the main part of the sub.

"*What?*" Verity says, voice an octave lower than a shout.

Ash takes the tablet back from Bracken and nods. "The mech. His people didn't just place a mobile EMP, but also a bug. I found it while the call was going on." He holds up a slim, sliver strip. No larger than Ig's pinky nail. "I disabled it, resulting in losing comms with him."

"So," Miles says. "He can't track us now."

"No," Ash says, then sighs. "You know, I wasn't so tech savvy until I joined up with you guys, right?"

Bracken claps Ash on the back. "Thanks, man. Really. You've helped so much in such little time."

Ash shrugs, holds up a wrist with thin, pink scars. "Like I said before, I had good motivation."

Ig nods.

"Ig," Verity says. "Don't believe what that asshole says. There isn't a cure. But the samples we have might—"

"Be bullshit," Ig finishes for her and laughs. "How do we even know anything? What if Murdock is telling the truth?"

"Because," Ash says, giving her a withering look at her. "That's what he does. He lies and twists the truth. He wants you to bring the samples alone, so he can take them and kill you and your mom." He waves the tablet. "Unless she's already dead."

"Which wouldn't surprise me with that asshole," Miles says.

"What did you just say?" Ig's flashes on Miles.

He sighs. "Ig, look, there's no telling what he might do."

Ig storms toward him. "You don't know! You don't know if those fucking samples will work. None of you do! You're all just guessing and this entire mission was bullshit!"

"Hun." Verity places a gentle hand on Ig's shoulder. "Calm down. We're on your side. If Leon says—"

"She's bullshit too." She spins. "Where's the mech? I'm deploying."

"Like hell you are." Leon steps around a large mound of crates.

Ig pauses. "How the hell did you get here?"

"I've been at the monitors and comms here the entire time. Locked in. Separate room from controls."

Ig huffs a breath, flaps her arms. "That's great and all, but I gotta go now." She starts forward and Leon pulls a gun from the inside of her jacket and points it at Ig.

"No. You don't. Murdock Jones is a snake. A liar. A criminal. Evil in every sense of the word. Didn't Anna ever speak of him?"

"Hardly," Ig says. "Only time she did was when…" She trails off, memories flooding in.

"*He's killing animals, Ig,*" Anna said once, tears in her eyes. "*He's killing them and bringing them back to life like zombies, only they're smart and they…they…he makes these things hunt people down he doesn't like.*"

The memories shuffle.

"*I think he killed my mom. Oh, God, he was smiling when she died in the hospital. I overheard him in the hall, too. Talking to one of his goons. Know what he said? He said he wanted her brain and nervous system taken out and placed in something. I can't remember what it's called, but Ig, it's like a robot or something!*"

Shuffle.

"*He lies, baby. He lied about Mom. He lied about what he's doing in that warehouse across town. He's lied about everything. He's a liar and I think he's going to send me away to school because I know too much, and he needs me out of the way. Says I can get a degree and come back to work for him. You believe that?*"

Now, Leon says, "That's what I thought." She holsters the sidearm and sighs. Her face softens. "Ignia, this is how he's lived all his life. Deflection and diversion. It's how he became so wealthy and powerful. He's good at what he does. Only way to know he's full of complete shit is to look back on his history."

All the drive to leave the sub withers inside Ig. She steps back, holding her arms up chest level, until her back thumps into a pipe. It's hot, but she doesn't move away from it right away. Instead, she lets the heat sink through her shirt and burn her skin. With a wince of pain, she finally steps away and finds her way to the seats across from the pods. Here she sits, not sure what to do or say.

Ready to give up.

Bracken hunkers down in front of her. His gaze fixes on her eyes. His own, a deep blue and kind. Yes. She sees complete kindness in those eyes of his.

"We do everything together, okay? We get the samples to base, then we'll plan our next move. You won't go alone."

Tears well in her eyes, obscuring her vision. "What…what about my mom?"

"Let's hope he hasn't done what Miles thinks he's done. Sometimes, all we have is hope. Let that light guide you. Your mom will be okay."

She's not sure if she believes him or not, but what other choice does she have?

Going in by herself, maybe Miles is right. Maybe Murdock will take the samples and order Ig and Mom killed. If—

It's like an explosion. Ig flies out of the seat, crashing into Bracken and they both slam onto the floor. Alarms blare. Bracken is helping her up when the world quakes again. The force knocks her off her feet. Ig is tossed into the seat sideways, knocking the wind out of her. She falls to the floor, grunting for air.

"What the shit?" Miles shouts. "Does Murdock have another sub?"

"He might, but—" Ash is cut off by another jolt.

Everything goes flying. Ig's head smacks against something. She's not even sure what, but pain bashes through her skull all the same. There's a moment of bright, white light, followed by chaotic agony rampaging through her head.

Over the speaker, cutting through the alarms, Leon says, "It's Mother! Bracken, Miles, Verity. Deploy and plant the explosives. She has detached from her egg-sack. Offspring are closing in."

Someone helps Ig into a seat and buckles the harness, though she's not sure who through the white fog in her mind. Verity, maybe?

"Sub can't take many more hits like those," Bracken shouts. "Let's go."

Once Ig's mind clears a bit, she soon finds herself alone and staring at a cryo-pod. The others are already getting ready for deployment.

She unbuckles the harness.

"Ignia," Leon announces through the speakers. "Stay put. They'll take care of it."

"I can help."

"No. You can't. You completed your mission. They haven't. This will be over soon. Just relax."

But she can't and darts out of the seat anyway.

"Ignia! Return to your seat!"

She ignores Leon and runs to the deployment bay. There she finds the three of them getting into their sleek, blue mechs.

Bracken pauses. "Go buckle in, Ig. We'll be right back."

"You don't get it," Ig shouts over the alarms. "She talks."

"So, we'll ignore her," Miles says.

"It's not that easy," Ig says. "She gets in your head. I think that's why I believed Murdock. She planted that seed."

They all glance at each other.

Finally, Bracken says, "Keep your wits about you. Like Miles said, we ignore her."

"Aren't you listening?" Ig asks. "You can try ignoring her all you want, but she'll find a way in. She's that powerful."

"I think we'll be okay," Bracken says. "Buckle in. We'll be back before you know it."

Ash stands at the deployment button and presses it when the three are ready. They step into the deployment area, room, whatever, and he presses the button again. The door slips shut.

It doesn't take long before deployment happens. Probably they're already cruising through the water toward Mother. Ready to plant the charges and blow her to bits for Team Two to clean up. That's if, of course, they even make it to Mother without being eaten by her offspring.

Ash nods. "We need to help Ben at the guns. Deter as many of those things as we can."

"I should be out there," Ig says. "My mech is stronger. Maybe if I can—"

"Leon would have me shut it down the moment you got in." Ash runs his hands through his shaggy, dark hair. "It also holds the samples. If something went wrong, we'd lose everything. Can't risk it."

He starts away from the deployment bay, and she follows.

"Well, we could take the samples out. Leave them here."

"No. They're cryogenically frozen inside the mech. If the samples are allowed to thaw, it might complicate cellular structure. Contamination might happen. We need the samples pure for testing and development."

Ig frowns. "Huh?" She shakes her head. "Never mind."

He stops, faces her. "The purer the samples, the better chance we have at a cure for your mom."

"Why is she top priority?"

He smiles. "Thank Leon. She put your mom at the top of the pile. The very first to be given a cure, once it's found. Even before we begin to distribute to hospitals around the world."

Ig's breath catches in her throat. She coughs, feeling like an ass for nearly siding with Murdock when Leon has given Ig's mom top priority.

"But," she says, "you're not sure if there's a cure in those samples, right?"

Ash turns away, continues walking. "No guarantee, like I've said before. But, according to topical data and internal graphs of Mother, it appears very likely. Otherwise, I would've been against this mission from the start."

She follows, not sure what to say, mind reeling.

Murdock offers a cure, or so he says. He's a billionaire, so it's possible he bought one of the so-called cures the big-name doctors and scientists say they have. But, what if they're all lying too, just to make more money? Isn't that how the world works now?

And if their cure is genuine…then how come no one, even the news, has spoken about anyone being cured?

She's never really thought about this until now.

All she knew before was one needed to be rich, or damn near, to afford a cure.

Yet, there are no testimonies confirming this "cure" actually works.

Shit, how come she's never thought about that before? Maybe in the back of her mind, but not like this.

CHAPTER 18

Ig follows Ash up a short flight of steps to a small, dome-like room.

Ben taps on a monitor, pushes off, and glides across the room on his chair to another monitor. He taps something there and moves to the center panel with the largest monitor. On the screen is Mother in most of her entirety.

"'Bout time someone came up here to help," Ben blurts and swivels around in his chair, arms crossing. "And everyone calls *me* the asshole."

Ash grunts. "You *are* the asshole." He wheels over another chair. "But a useful one. How are they doing?"

"Oh," Ben says, hawks back, and spits a glob of greenish phlegm on the floor. "So far so good. No one's died yet, if that's what ya wanna know."

"Great. How many offspring are near?"

"Eight, so far from what I can tell. None close enough to kill, though." He turns and winks at Ig. "By the way, lady, you should be thankin' me. Shot 'n' killed six of them bastards while ya were out there. All of 'em 'bout ready to make you their evening snack."

Ig musters a smile. "Thanks."

Ben gives a nod. "Of course. Might be an asshole, but I'm on y'alls side."

Ig still doesn't like him, but at least he seems relatively good-hearted. Relatively...

Through a speaker in the room, Leon says, "Ignia, please take a seat. Ben and Ash will instruct you on what to do. ETA for collision is one minute. Keep your ears and eyes open and shoot anything that gets close enough."

"Aye-aye, Captain," Ben shouts.

"Don't be a smartass, Benjamin."

He blows out a breath, cheeks puffing. "Fine then." He swivels back to the monitors, taking the one on the far right.

Ash says, "Grab a chair and take this left monitor, Ig. It fits into tracks. If there's turbulence, the tracks lock so we won't go flying."

"Didn't work a little bit ago," Ben spouts. "Got thrown right out of my chair. Need a damn seatbelt."

Ash ignores him and points at a third chair hooked into tracks against the far wall.

Ig grabs the chair and places it on the track in front of the long panel of monitors. It clicks into place. She sits down and glances at Ash.

"Um, what am I supposed to be doing?"

He stares at blue specks as they jet toward Mother on his monitor. Off-handedly, he says, "You have the left-side turret. Watch the screen. If anything is sensed within range, gun it down. If it's too strong, I'll shoot a couple torpedoes."

"Damn..."

"Point is to try and protect our people out there in the Devil's Trench," Ben says.

Ig frowns at the screen in front of her. So far, there's a large object about a mile away. Too far to shoot at. Other than that...nothing.

"They're planting the explosives now," Ash says. He's so focused on his monitor, Ig can't help but admire him.

Despite his nerdy demeanor, Ash cares about everyone.

Intrigued, Ig glances at his monitor. She watches three sleek, blue mechs firing objects at Mother in various spots. They dodge tentacles and snapping mouths, moving with confidence and ease while they spin and dart back and forth. So much faster than her mech and she now understands why, save for the samples, she'd be deadweight out there.

Watching them is like watching blue fairies dart around a giant.

A sharp beep draws her attention back to her monitor.

Where there had only been one creature out there, now there's two. Very big, although she's not entirely sure what size her gun won't stop.

Both lifeforms are one hundred meters and closing.

"Two big ones moving into range," Ig says, even if she doesn't need to. It's better to have Ash with her and watchful than assuming what to do next.

"If they come within fifty meters," he says, "Open fire."

"Um, okay." She stares at the monitor. Green blobs floating toward the center where she assumes they are.

Eighty meters, the monitor reads.

"So, how do I aim and fire the guns?" she asks.

"Shit," Ash says. "Forgot about that. Under the panel is a control stick. Aim using that and fire using the trigger."

"So," she says, "like a video game?"

"More or less," Ash says, "yes. Just remember, no closer than fifty meters. Blast the hell out of them if they get to that point."

The monitor says the creatures are sixty meters away and closing.

She grips the control stick and the monitor changes. Suddenly, she's gaping at the creatures themselves and not just green blobs.

"Gods," she manages through numb lips. "What the hell are those?"

Ash leans over, glaring at the monitor. It takes him less than a minute. "Hybrids, by the look. They each have characteristics of *Dunkleosteus*, *Basilosaurus*, and..." He trails off, frown deepening.

"And what?" Ig asks, heart hammering.

"Looks like...a *Tylosaurus*. A species of mosasaur, only much larger." He looks at Ig. "Too large to stop them with your guns."

"I should still shoot them, though, right? I mean, to help?"

"No," Ash says, frantically tapping on a lit panel in front of him. "I'll hit them with a torpedo each. If they don't change course, yes, I want you to open fire until I get reloaded. Automatic reload for torpedoes take longer than a turbo recycles for the lasers. About a minute each."

"Okay," she says, settling back a bit.

She fights the tightening in her chest. Her hand creeps toward the pocket holding the inhaler. But, miraculously, the steel bands around her chest loosen. A few slow, deep breaths, and it goes away completely. Sometimes the asthma can be controlled without an inhaler. Few and far between, but it happens.

"Sighting in offspring one," Ash says.

Unlike Ig's and Ben's control stick, Ash's stick is on the panel. Leaning forward, fully focused on the large screen in front of him, he moves the control stick up, taps it down, then leans it to the right. His thumb presses a blue button near the top of the control stick. The floor under Ig's boots trembles.

"Gotcha," Ash says and pulls the red trigger.

Ig looks to her monitor just as a bubbly, white gash cuts through the water and to the monstrosity speeding right for Bracken, Miles, and Verity.

She draws in a breath. Holds it.

The torpedo is a direct hit and the explosion is so massive it blots the creature out in a cloud of darkness and trillions of bubbles. For at least a full minute, there's nothing but that giant cloud rising slowly toward the surface.

Ash never moves. He keeps his gaze fixed on the monitor screen.

Breath still held, she lets it out in a torrent. Neither notice. Both men are glued to the monitors. She returns her sight back to her own screen just in time to watch the enormous monster sink, the ruined stump where its head once dominated inking the water a deep scarlet.

"Where's the other one?" Ben asks.

"Might've taken off after what we did to its brother there," Ash says.

"It'll be back," Ben mutters. "They always circle 'round."

"Maybe." Ash straightens a bit. "Sensors and radar aren't showing any threats now. Maybe this will be quicker than I thought."

Ig blinks at her monitor. "Why isn't Mother trying to stop them?"

"Who? Bracken?"

She nods. "She's just letting them plant the explosives. Doesn't that seem weird to you?"

"Maybe she's giving up," Ben says. "Or she's just had enough of this existence."

"No," Ig says. "She likes what she is and what she's doing." Her frown deepens.

"How do you know that?" Ash asks.

"She talked to me out there. Well, in my head, but you know what I mean."

"Telepathy," Ash says.

"Yeah. That. I think." A shiver trickles through her. "It was unnerving."

"Shit," Ben interjects. "I bet."

"What did she say to you?"

Ig, still staring at the monitor, says, "That the samples won't work, mostly. And if I gave in to her, she'd give me my girlfriend, Anna, back." Finally, she faces Ash. "Anna was Murdock Jones' daughter."

Both Ash and Ben gape at her. Neither of them say anything. Silence draws out.

It's Ben who finally breaks the quiet. "Wait, what?"

"I know," Ash says.

"How the hell do you know, and I don't?" Ben barks.

Ash swivels in his chair to look at Ben. "Because Leon didn't want you to know."

"He does now," Leon spurts from the speakers. "Thanks, Ash. Look alive, your three. Sensors are indicating an influx of energies."

"From Mother?" Ash asks.

"Possibly, though the source is elusive."

Ash sighs. "So, what do we do?"

"Mother is docile right now because, from what I've seen through data…she's giving birth. Every fifteen minutes, she births offspring. I say we finish with the charges and blow her to Hell before the fifteen minutes are up."

"Sounds great," Ben blurts. "But when do ya know that is?"

"We have four minutes left," Leon says. "In two, I'll call them back. They'll need to hyper speed back and we'll be exposed for one minute."

Ash nods at Ig. "Which means, we're the only line of defense. Shoot to kill."

"More or less," Leon says. "We'll also be exposed and an easier target for Mother and her offspring. Be vigilant."

"Aye-aye, Capt—"

"Benjamin, I swear to God if you call me captain one more time in such a manner, I will come up there and rearrange your insides with a taser."

Ben flashes a smile at Ig and Ash. "She loves me."

"Loathe is more like it. Man your station, dimwit." Faint click, and Leon is off the air.

Ben swivels to his monitor, chuckling.

A counter appears at the bottom Ig's monitor in red numbers; same with Ash's. She can't quite see Ben's but she's sure it's the same. The counter has already begun to tick away from four minutes. 4:00, 3:59, 3:58, and so on.

"At the two-minute mark," Ash says, "shoot anything that comes into range and don't stop until it's either badly wounded or dead."

"Sounds like a video game I played once," Ben spouts. "You were this guy who had to save an entire army from—"

"I've played it," Ash mutters. "Get ready."

"Well, shit. Excuse me for being nice for a change." Ben mocks a frustrated sigh and looks at his screen, thankfully falling silent.

3:20, 3:19…

Bracken, Miles, and Verity continue planting the charges.

Ig leans forward a bit, gaze drifting back and forth, searching for anything emerging from the darkness of the trench. Like a rookie fighter pilot, she clutches the control stick, heart thrashing about in her chest.

3:00, 2:59…

Her breathing grows louder, faster. No matter how much she tries to keep it from doing so. Like clockwork, those old iron bands close around her chest, cinching tighter. This time, taking slow, deep breaths aren't working.

"Use it," Ash says.

"Huh?"

"Your inhaler. Use it while you have some time."

She doesn't argue and inhales two puffs, holding her breath each time to make sure the medicine takes hold.

"One of those samples," Ash says, "might cure you too."

Ig snorts. "I doubt it. But it'd be nice."

"There's already a cure from Big Pharma."

"Yeah, but only millionaires can afford it. Like the ALS cure and cancer cures."

He nods. "Yeah. The last two you mentioned don't really exist, though."

As she figured earlier, it's all a sham. "So, that's how you all knew Murdock was full of shit."

"Yep. And why the cures are so highly priced. They know only a small percentage of people could ever afford the faux cures. Asthma cure, though...that's real. Still about one million dollars for a shot, but at least it's—here we go."

Ig blinks, glances at her monitor just as the counter falls on the two-minute mark.

Bracken, Miles, and Verity stop planting charges and turn toward the sub.

"Let's go home," Ash whispers.

Blue light shimmers under the feet of their sleek mechs, but—

It comes out of nowhere. There is no warning. No alarm. No blinking lights. A large, black tentacle lashes out of Mother, smacking all three aside like flies.

"Oh, fuck." Ben almost shoots out of his chair.

"Calm down," Ash says. "Don't shoot her. Might hit one of the charges and our people are still too close."

Ig gasps, watching helplessly while all three tumble into darkness. "I can't see them anymore."

"Far enough away, then," Ben says, leaning forward.

"No," Ash nearly shouts. "I said calm down. Need them to be on their way to the sub before opening fire." He leans back. "Leon? Any communication from Bracken?"

A slight pause. "No. I've lost all tracking on them as well."

"Shit," Ash says.

Ig, staring at the absolute black of the Devil's Trench, says, "Let me go."

"What?" Ash snaps a frown at her.

She takes a breath. "Give me ten minutes. You see us, turn the cloaks off, and—"

"Ignia," Leon says, frustration making her voice a tad shrill. "You know that's not an option. Those samples—"

Ig slams a fist on the panel. "The samples will be fine! Let me try to help them. For gods sake, they *need* help!" She stands.

"Ig," Ash says. "They might already be dead."

She glowers at him. "Is this who we are? We just give up on people because something is too hard? I thought the Resistance was the opposite of the Government. I thought you're here to save lives and stop fascism."

She shakes her head and turns away from Ash. "Right now, I'm not seeing any of that." She tromps down the steps to the main sub floor.

Through all the speakers, Leon says, "We *are* trying to save lives, Ignia. Those samples will save many. And for free. We aren't even asking for a profit."

Ig sighs and starts toward the rear of the sub. "Yeah, well, I'm not about abandoning people we're supposed to care about."

"They knew the risks," Leon says. "If they're...compromised, they did it to save lives."

"You're talking sacrifices. That's not what this is supposed to be about." Ig's pace increases. She's almost to the deployment area.

"What do you think this entire mission what about, Ignia? Why would we all jet out to the deepest ocean and confront a creature roughly the size of a small mountain and her vicious offspring, if not as a sacrifice for humanity?"

Ig stops at her mech. The hulking thing is scarred from teeth, though still a nice, shiny silver. It's secured to a beam with heavy straps.

"If those samples are lost," Leon continues, "your mother won't be cured. Everyone suffering with ALS won't be cured. Cancer will continue to kill children, mothers...and fathers. You must realize how important the samples are in that mech."

"I do," Ig says. "But you need to realize how much those lives out there mean to me too."

To this, Leon says nothing and falls silent.

She figures out how to take the straps securing the mech to the beam off and climbs in. She almost hates how comfortable it feels. Like sitting in an old, much-loved recliner. Ig shouldn't feel this way, she knows, and yet she does.

Mechanical armor shouldn't be comfortable.

How many hours are left before she's supposed to meet Murdock? Four? Three? She shoves it out of her mind for now and seals the hatch. The mech whirs to life. Air whooshes in. All the lights flicker on.

The speakers fill with both Leon's and Ash's voices.

"We don't know where they are," Leon says.

"She has a point, though," Ash says.

"Fire a torpedo into Mother. The explosion will trigger the charges and we can get back to the mainland."

"Look," Ash says, "I know they signed that waiver of yours, but they're still people. We can't just let them die out there."

"I care about them just as much as you," Leon says, voice straining, barely keeping it together. "But what do you think they'd want? Us risking those samples to save them, or blow Mother up and warp drive to the mainland?"

To this, Ash says nothing.

Doesn't matter. Now that she's in the mech, they can't stop her unless they have an EMP. Which they might have, but she doesn't care.

Ig maneuvers the mech toward the deployment area, not entirely sure how she's going to open and close the door to the deployment room by herself and not compromise everyone one else on the sub though working on a plan. She needs string. If she can tie a string to a heavy pipe, or something, once she's inside the deployment room, she can pull the string and, hopefully, the pipe or whatever will fall away from the button. Then, maybe...

"Make it quick," Ash says, striding to the panel near the deployment door. "I'll give you six minutes, not ten. We'll be exposed for only a minute and a half. Can't go on longer than that. If we disappear, it's over. I'm sorry."

"What do you mean it's over?"

He steps onto the platform in front of the deployment panel. "Leon won't let us stay any longer. And yes, I know you're listening, just can't respond." He pauses, sighs at Ig. "Sorry for what you're about to receive."

Ig frowns, not really sure what he's talking about when Leon's voice trails out of the speakers in a harsh torrent.

"Ignia, you shut the mech down now! We can't afford to lose everything. If Bracken and the other two are still alive, they'll find their way to the mainland. Right now, it's about protecting those samples at all cost. Even Bracken would agree with me. Shut it down and let's go home!"

And when Ig doesn't respond...

"Let's save your mother."

Ig stops. She opens her mouth, blood pounding through her temples. Finally, she manages, "I am."

Ash places a hand on the panel and the deployment door whispers open. He nods. "Kick some ass."

She draws in a breath, nods, and enters the deployment room.

The door shuts behind her and the floor opens, sending her sinking like a boulder into the Devil's Trench.

"Stabilize," she says and the mech halts its descent.

"Ignia," Leon shouts through the speakers. "You're not combat ready! Get your ass back here!"

"I'm doing what's right." Then she switches off comms, but leaving her tracking on. She needs all her wits about her now and someone screaming at her from speakers less than five inches from her head will do nothing but distract her.

Ig positions the mech and faces Mother. She keeps turning, aiming herself in the direction Bracken and his team disappeared. She sucks in a puff from the inhaler, stows it, and says, "Full forward thrust."

The mech blasts through the water. She veers away from Mother, heart hammering. If those tentacles are really long, she might be in trouble.

As it turns out, however, even as one lashes out at her, it misses by several meters. She adjusts her trajectory and dives a bit. The high-density lamps on the mech slice through the darkness. Away from Mother, it's like running blind through a minefield. The lamps cut through the black, though only a few meters ahead.

"Mild thrust," she says and the mech slows to a speed she can wrap her head around.

She makes sure all the sensors are working and, after some trial error, reconfigures size recognition. This might put her at risk of larger sizes, like Mother's offspring, but what matters most right now is finding Bracken, Miles, and Verity.

Verity. The woman's smile floating through Ig's mind still stokes heat in Ig's chest. There's nothing more, except for curing Mom, Ig desires more than to see Verity's smile again. Just one more smile and...

A spark of blue glints at her not far ahead. She wants to full forward thrust, yet that might end up with her speeding right by without realizing it. So, she keeps the speed mild. Gradually, the blue glint shines in the lamps until, finally, revealing a shape. Still meters away, but...

Ig turns the comms on, though at low volume. To her surprise, Leon isn't spewing anything from the speakers. A soft buzz filters through, and that's all.

She grapples onto the blue figure, not sure if it's Verity, Bracken, or Miles. Doesn't matter, though she wishes she had a tethering system. Something to hook onto each person as she finds them. As it is...she must hold the person while searching for the other two. If they're all unconscious, or disabled, how's she supposed to get them to the sub?

Maybe she should've thought this through a bit more, though it's not like she had time to either.

"Verity?" She checks all her monitors, but they only show her the darkness of the Devil's Trench.

Verity doesn't respond.

"Bracken?"

Nothing.

Ig sighs. "Miles?"

A crackle finds its way through the silence. "Y-Yeah."

Her heart jackhammers. "Miles? It's Ig. Where are you?"

"I...I don't know. What happened?'

"One of Mother's tentacles happened."

He grunts. "Lovely. Think she knocked ten years' worth of memories out of me."

"At least you're still alive."

"Right. You find anyone else?"

She looks at the limp, metallic blue mech in her larger mech arms. "Yeah, but not sure who."

"Doesn't matter." Another grunt. "I see your lights."

And before she has time to search, four high-density lights glare through the dark at her. They dim a bit and in no time, a sleek, blue mech cruises up to her. It hovers a few feet away.

"I'll search around and try hailing them," Miles says. "We can't be too far away from each other."

"Okay," she says, never feeling so useless in her life.

Miles darts away. Through the speakers, he calls for Verity and Bracken over and over.

Ig glances around. A shiver snakes along her spine. The darkness of the Devil's Trench creeps, closing in around her. A formless oblivion ready to feast.

Monsters come in many forms, but those which are formless cannot be stopped. No bullet, laser, or torpedo will kill them.

Because the darkness is eternal.

CHAPTER 19

"H-Hello?"

Ig sucks in a breath. She looks around but finds no blue mech nearby.

"Hey! Where are you?" It takes all of her will not to shout this.

"Um…in your arms."

The blue mech in her arms moves and waves a hand at her.

"Holy shit," Ig manages.

"Missed you too," Verity says.

VERITY!

Ig wants to kiss her, but, of course, that's not possible. Instead, a smile beams on her face. Tears of joy well in her eyes. She blinks them away and they trickle down her cheeks.

"Miles," Ig says. "I—"

"Open comms, Ig," Miles says in a calm tone. "I heard. Welcome back, Verity."

"Thanks, I guess," Verity says. "Think I liked the nothingness better than this hell."

"I hear that," Miles says.

Verity maneuvers out of Ig's mech arms and hovers in front of her. "So, where's Bracken?"

"Still haven't found him," Miles says.

"He can take care of himself." Leon sounds on the verge of murder. "He knows what he's doing. Get back to the sub. I'm detonating the charges in—"

A loud squeal ravages Ig's ears. Then…static. The static holds for a second or two before dying in silence.

"Oh…shit…" Verity says, blue suit gleaming from sudden light.

"What?" Ig frowns.

"Turn around."

Ig does and immediately squints against the brilliance. "Oh, my gods…" It's all she manages once the glare dims.

An explosion. It's the only way she can describe it. A core of light and hundreds of red hot shards arcing in every direction and sizzling into the dark trench. A massive creature, something she can't place by looking at it, sweeps by. Something with enormous jaws and teeth. It's all she catches before it disappears beyond the light.

"Mission's been compromised," Miles says. "You two, help me find Bracken. He's the only one who can detonate the charges."

Verity says, "Did it…are they…?"

"All dead," Miles says. "Now *move*."

When Ig turns to face her, Verity cruises off to the right.

"What if he fell deeper into the trench?" Ig asks.

"Only mech capable of going that deep is yours," Miles says. "But let's search up here first. Eighty-meter radius."

After some time, the search is fruitless. They find each other, no one saying anything at first. Hope dwindles.

Perhaps Bracken was hit the hardest and died on impact.

This is the horror which infiltrates Ig's mind. A broken back or neck. Bracken floating, either dead or dying, or completely paralyzed in the deep darkness of the Devil's Trench.

No. She can't leave him like that.

"He must've fallen into the deeper trench," Miles says finally.

"Either that or taken away by a current," Verity adds.

"Possible," Miles says. "But my sensors aren't picking up any current strong enough to carry him."

Ig sucks in a puff from her inhaler, blows out a breath, and says, "I'll check deeper."

Both are quiet for a moment, until finally Miles says, "Be careful. We don't know what, if anything, is down there. Could be a rejected offspring, for all we know."

"You think that happens? Rejected offspring?" Ig asks.

"Who knows? All I'm saying is be cautious down there."

Ig sighs and positions herself to dive. Her heart batters at the walls of her chest.

Aimed downward, she says, "Full forward thrust."

The darkness barely parts before the lights. At any given time, her sight barely reaches twenty feet in front of her. At this speed, she's more or less running blind.

Around one thousand-six hundred feet deep, she calls for the mech to decrease to the mild thrusters. The trench is absolute darkness. So much so, her high-density lamps can't sufficiently cut through.

She might have shot right by Bracken, even if the sensors didn't pick anything up.

Pulsing backward, she calls, "Bracken?"

Nothing.

She turns slowly, heart thudding. Her breathing remains steady. Her nerves pause. Everything falls still inside her for a moment.

"Ig…"

It's like getting kickstarted. Her heart stutters to life. She sucks in a breath and it's as though electricity crackles and snaps over her skin. "Bracken?"

"Yeah. Where—?" He makes a strained noise. "Where are you?"

"One thousand five-hundred feet."

His breathing is a wheezy mess through the speakers. Sounds worse than she does during an asthma attack. For the longest time, all he does is try to breathe.

"Are you okay?" Ig asks.

"Got hit pretty hard by...something. Not sure what. Think it damaged a couple of the intakes that turns water into breathable air."

"Shit," Ig says. "What do I do?"

"Get...just get me to the sub."

A breath catches in her throat like a sharp fishbone. She coughs and manages, "It's gone."

A long pause. "What?"

"Something..." A shudder passes through her.

"Something, what?"

"I don't know what it was," Ig says. "Something really big, almost as big as Mother. It chomped right through the sub."

Once more, Bracken goes quiet. She waits, but after a couple full minutes, she can't take it anymore.

"You still there?"

He sucks in a wheezy breath. "Yeah. When we make it to the mainland, we'll need to set a memorial for all those on the sub." He only pauses a couple seconds. "Miles? Verity?"

"They're waiting for us above the trench."

Bracken sighs. "Okay. I think I see you now. I'm going to pulse up but will need you to carry me the rest of the way."

"Just hurry up," Ig says. "It's creepy down here."

And it is. Even the strong lights of her mech barely penetrate the darkness of the trench. Anything might be lurking in this thick, obsidian soup, even if her sensors aren't blaring. Maybe there's something beyond the sensors. A monster of the deep slowly creeping closer and closer. And maybe the sensors can't detect it. Maybe it blends in with the walls of the trench as it slips through the darkness toward her...

Madness, as it happens to sailors suck at sea for months on end, also slinks its way into divers. And that's what she is right now, essentially. A deep-sea diver. Mech or not. She hasn't spent much time in the deep, but that doesn't matter either. Because she's not formally trained to deal with it is all she has. Trained to extract blood. Check. Trained to diffuse the mind from the claustrophobic darkness of the deep? Nope.

Bracken rises out of the darkness of the Devil's Trench before her, blue mech gleaming in the lights so bad she squints against the glare.

Once her eyes adjust, she mutters, "Oh, shit..."

"As bad as I feel?" Bracken asks.

"Worse," she says, gaze drifting over his mech. The entire left side is a wrinkled, creased ruin. She shakes her head. "How can we fix it, so you can breathe?"

After a couple wheezes, he manages, "Can't. I'm gonna have to conserve air until we get out of the water."

Ig blinks. "What about the second team coming in for clean up?"

"Yeah. Let's do what we came here for first."

"Okay."

The boots of Bracken's mech glow bright blue and he shoots upward.

"Full upward thrust," she says and soon paces Bracken.

Together, they rise out of the depths of the trench, soon meeting up with Miles and Verity. As they cruise back toward Mother, an idea surfaces in her mind.

***

"Let me get this straight," Miles says. "You want us to be *bait*?"

"Well—"

"Because, if so, you're just as fruitbatty as ol' Bracken here."

"I like it," Bracken says.

"Of course *you* do. That's what I'm saying."

"How, though?" Verity asks. "Some of those things are faster than our mechs."

Ig opens her mouth, closes it. Verity makes a good point. They float, about eight hundred yards from Mother. If the creature knows they're close, it gives no sign.

It takes her a while, but Ig answers Verity's question. "We're smarter than them, right?"

"Well, technically," Ash says and a new blue mech joins their little circle, "they might be more intelligent than we think."

"Holy shit," Miles says. "How they hell did you—?"

"I was suiting up to come help Ig when that thing bit into the sub." Ash turns to Ig. "You did the right thing, by the way. Leon wasn't thinking clearly."

"What...the hell did I miss?" Bracken says between wheezes.

"You," Ash says, "need to get to Sub Two. They should be coming soon."

"Shut...up. What happened...to Leon?"

Ash sighs. "Ig here, she took it upon herself to suit up and come out here to help you all. Leon wanted to blow Mother up, then go find you."

"Leon was pissed," Ig says. "But I couldn't leave you guys out here. Didn't think that's what the Resistance is about. We don't just leave our people."

"Exactly," Ash says. "What Leon wanted was against everything the Resistance stands for."

"Damn..." Bracken says.

Ash sighs. "It happened so fast. I couldn't get her into the reserve mech. I tried. Couldn't find Ben and the two pilots..."

"Man," Miles says. "It's okay. Really. Bunch of shit, what happened. You tried and that's what counts."

A resounding yes from Ig, Verity, and Bracken.

"Anyway," Ash says. "First order of business is to get Bracken to Sub Two."

"No," Bracken manages, coughs. "We follow Ig's plan."

"I didn't catch all of it," Ash says.

"Ig?" Bracken wheezes.

She clears her throat. "Okay. So, we gather the offspring so they're close to Mother. Once we have as many as we can round up, Bracken detonates the charges. Hopefully fatally injuring or killing them all."

Everyone is silence for a moment.

Ash says, "So, like bait?"

"That's what I'm *saying*," Miles shouts.

"But...it's a good plan," Bracken says.

"Bracken," Ash says. "With the condition of your mech, you're not able to do any of that."

"We follow Ig's plan." Bracken's tone is firm before he falls into a fit of coughing.

Ig nods, knowing what has to be done. "You will hang back, Bracken. Once we have the offspring gathered, detonate."

"Only...one problem there..." he wheezes. It takes him a moment to finish. "You'll all...be compromised in the blast."

"Not if we coordinate," Ig says, firm. "Hang back. You're the only one who can detonate the charges."

Bracken doesn't say anything, nor do the others. She's not sure if they agree or not. But...

"You should be...the one hanging back," Bracken says. "You...have the samples."

"She can still maneuver better," Miles says.

"And breathe better," Ash adds.

"And think better," Verity spouts.

Bracken makes a sound close to a grunt. "Y'all calling me old?"

"Hardly," Miles says. "Your mech is all messed up and we need you around to detonate—"

"Yes," Verity interjects, "You're old. Now do what Ig says."

"I…didn't mean to—"

"I know," Verity says. "But, really, Ig's plan is a good one."

After this, everyone filters into utter silence for a while. Even Ig fails to find anything to say.

Finally, Bracken says, "Okay. Longest distance I can be from Mother is one thousand feet to detonate. Ig, you tell me when."

A heavy weight thumps upon her shoulders like a large slab of beef. Even in the mech, she hunches.

It's time to step up or shut up.

"Alright," she says, after the shock wears off a bit. "So, we gather as many of the offspring as possible."

"Some are smarter than you realize," Ash inserts. "We need a maneuver plan that's unpredictable."

"Right," Miles says. He's quiet for a handful of seconds, then… "Okay, here's what we do. Verity, you stick with Ig. Her mech is bulkier and slower and she'll need someone to watch her back. I want you two on the right flank of Mother."

"She has flanks?" Verity asked. "Because she looks like she goes on forever."

"She's very large," Ash says, "but she has a body of about one thousand feet wide by six thousand tall."

"No way," Ig says. "It's not even that deep here."

"Correct. Not here, but a good portion of her is in the deeper half of the trench."

Mind reeling, she tries to envision the sheer enormity of Mother.

"The Devil's Trench is estimated at ten miles wide and stretches one hundred more," Ash says. "Its depth, though…" He snorts. "Shit if I know. It's unfathomable, so to speak."

"Hey," Miles says, "thanks for the geography lesson, buddy, but can we get back to the mission?"

"Nah," Ash says. "Wanna know how the Devil's Trench opened up?"

After a chuckle, Miles replies, "God no! Shush."

"Well, I—"

Ash's words are bashed to the wayside when all the alarms in Ig's mech blares. Red lights flicker. The sudden change nearly stops her heart.

Through the blaring, Miles shouts, "Incoming! Left!"

Ig turns to the left…and freezes.

It's the massive thing that bit the sub in two and all she can see are the jaws and long, crooked teeth. Its maw is large enough to swallow a jetliner whole.

A blue flash in front of her and suddenly Miles, Verity, and Ash are blasting that giant mouth with lasers. They're fighting, and all she can do is float, barely breathing. Absently, she takes a quick puff from her inhaler. More like half a puff, since it's about empty.

Lovely, she thinks.

The monster's huge jaws snap shut, sending a shock wave through the water so strong it shoves Ig and the other backward. It dives into the deeper part of the trench and disappears.

"Jesus," Verity mutters. "And we're supposed to round things like that up?"

Ig opens her mouth, not entirely sure what she's going to say until it's out. "Yes. And we need to be quick."

"She's sending signals to her offspring," Ash says. "Once again, like a queen bee to the drones and soldiers. They'll fight to the death for her. When she sees us as a real threat…things will get crazy."

"So," Miles says, "Ig and Verity, you take the right flank. Ash and I will take the left. We shoot at Mother from seventy meters away. Until she calls them all in. Once that happens, my friends, it's game on. Lead them all as close to Mother as you can and rapid pulse—full forward thrust for you, Ig—the hell away. When we're a good one hundred meters away, I'll give Bracken the order to detonate."

"I can only be…one hundred meters…for the signal," Bracken manages.

Everyone pauses for a couple seconds until finally Miles asks, "How far do we need to be and not get hit by the blasts?"

"At least eighty meters," Bracken says. "But…I don't know…for sure."

"Save your air," Ash interjects. "Can't have you passing out on us due to lack of oxygen, my friend."

"Yeah," Verity says. "I mean, if you die, how are we gonna blow sea monsters up and shit?"

Bracken laughs, coughs, and says, "Good point."

"So, Brack," Miles says.

"Call me Brack one more time…and I'll laser burst your ass."

A small chuckle. "My bad. Bracken. Get set up in the one-hundred-meter range." He sighs. "Everyone else, you know your positions. Don't start firing until I say so. When they swarm, immediately head for the front of Mother. As soon as we meet, get the hell out of there."

"Oo-rah," Verity says.

"Got it," Ig says.

"Let's go," Ash says.

And so, they part ways, Verity staying close to Ig while they speed through the water until the thousand-feet mark. Here, they slow to check out their position. To the left are the dark waters of the open ocean. Ahead, about forty meters, Mother shifts and wiggles her greenish, voluptuous self.

"Thirty more meters," Verity shouts. "Need to be seventy, like Miles said."

Ig follows Verity until they reach the seventy-meter mark. Here, she faces Mother. The moment she does, a familiar voice says, "This is not the way, Ignia." The voice of Mother. Feminine, yet, not really. To identify by voice there's certainly a nonbinary aspect at play.

Even so, she refuses to reply to Mother. Replying only leads to madness with such a creature.

Mother tries to smother this, but Miles breaks through with, "Fire!"

Ig aims and fires a steady beam into Mother while Verity slams the creature with heavy laser bursts.

"Just keep blasting her," Miles shouts. "She's trying to get into our heads. Ignore her. Do not stop firing."

"She talking to you, Ig?" Verity asks.

"Did a little. Not now."

"Okay, nothing here."

"Good."

Black and red wisps swirl out of Mother. No matter how much she and Verity shoot and cut through all that greenish flesh, nothing happens.

"She's talking to me," Miles says. "Ash. Hit me."

A loud crackle of static follows.

After a few seconds, Miles says, "Better. Okay. Keep the heat on this bitch."

Neither Verity nor Ig let up on the attack. The waters around Mother turn murky with bits of charred flesh and scorched blood. The assault is brutal, but oddly tame, compared to what Ig envisioned. Honestly, she didn't know what to expect, save for the carnage. Slicing and dicing. Scarlet obscures the waters where wounds don't quite get cauterized. It comes to a point where she just wishes for it to all end. No matter how much imbalance to the seas Mother serves, she's still a living creature. A very intelligent one at that and...

"You can stop this," Mother whispers in Ig's mind. So weak compared to before. The very slight of her voice makes Ig's heart ache a little. "I was here long before the dinosaurs. I was here before humans. I am the creator of the sea and if you let this happen…the sea shall die."

Imbalance? Suddenly, Ig isn't so sure.

"They will cut through my blubber soon," Mother whispers. "When they do, I will die."

"Then why don't you fight back?" Ig asks.

"Ig? That you?" Miles asks, sounding slightly distracted.

She doesn't answer him. Instead, she waits for Mother's response.

Eventually, Mother says, "Because…I'm currently giving birth."

Ig's heart stutters. She stops firing her laser. "Wh-What?"

"Most of my will is releasing my new baby into the sea. I can't signal my children to help. I can't fight back on my own in this state."

"Ig?" Verity asks. "Who are you talking to? And why aren't you shooting?"

Faint, but there, Bracken says, "Don't…listen to Mother, Ig. She's deceptive."

"Ig," Miles shouts. "I swear to God I'll destroy those samples myself if you believe what that bitch says."

"How the hell do either of you know that?" she asks. "Has she talked to you? Have there been tests done on it?"

"Ig," Bracken wheezes. "She spoke to me. She—"

"He's lying," Mother whispers. "I have never spoken to him. All he wants is to kill me, because he doesn't understand me."

"Why can't we just leave with the samples and let her be?" Ig asks.

"You know why," Ash says. "Trust me, her offspring will deplete the ocean's resources. And, depending, they might evolve and come onto land."

"He lies," Mother hisses.

"But, like before," Ig says, "you guys don't know. This is all a damn guess, isn't it?"

"Ig," Verity says. "You know better. Don't listen to her."

"I mean," Ig says. "How do we really know anything, right?"

"I don't," Verity says. "Ig, look at all the deaths her monsters have created so far. You really think she's telling you the truth? We've been through this already."

And they have. But still, what if there's a chance they're wrong?

"Evil is killing a mother," Mother says. "When all a mother wants is to live to see her children grow."

Despite everything, this tugs on Ig's heart. Images of her own mother flicker through her mind. Yes, evil is killing a mother and letting her children watch her die. This she knows well.

Verity is still shooting at Mother. No doubt, Miles and Ash are too.

"She will spin lies like a...spider spins webs," Bracken says. "Intricate and strong. She'll use...your sanity...against you."

"This is like that big fucking sea snake, Ig," Miles says. "It got in my head. It blacked me out, made me kill almost everyone aboard the minisub. That's what these things do. It's a damn game to them."

"Not...a game..." Bracken says. "Diversion."

"Bracken," Ash spouts. "For the last time, save your air."

Diversion...

The word tumbles around in Ig's head. Diversion. But what is Mother trying to divert her from? What...?

She turns the mech to the right and... "Oh. Oh shit."

"Huh?" Verity says, still blasting away at Mother.

They emerge from the murk of the open sea, her high-density lamps picking them out as they glide closer and closer. A few have those reflective deer eyes when the light touches them. More than a little eerie, a series of shivers trickle through her like ice water.

"Ig," Verity says. "What the hell are you...?" She falls silent for a couple seconds. Then, "Oh my God."

"What's going on over there?" Miles asks.

Ig tries to tell him, but only a mild whine leaks through her mouth.

"Look behind Mother," Verity says. "Bracken was right about the diversion."

There's only a second pause when Miles says, "Son of a bitch."

"She gathered them," Ash says. "We were so distracted cutting into her so she'd call for them we never realized she was waiting for just the right moment."

"And that moment is soon," Miles says. "They're just staring at us right now."

A low sigh fills Ig's head. "I could have had my children end all of you the moment you arrived. But did not. Because I believe in life, as all life should believe in itself. Up until now, I have been patient. This patience has grown very thin. Leave us be, and I spare everyone. If you do not..." Mother lets this hang in Ig's mind, though the threat is clear.

Ig shakes her head. "How do I know you're telling the truth?"

"Because I know about your mother, Ignia. I know what has happened and I care. This, and this only, is why I have been so lenient. Final warning. Get your friends to flee, and they shall all live."

Ig frowns. "How'd you know about my mom?"

"Your thoughts. I hear them over all the others."

"Why me?"

"Because you are of the people born of this part of Earth. You are one with the land and sea. Is it not so?"

"Ig?" Verity says. "Tell me you're not still talking to her."

"Shh," Ig says to Verity. "Hold on." She redirects herself to Mother. "Sure. But, we're all people of the earth. Why not talk to the others more?" A sudden revelation occurs to her. "Or do you feel like I'm the weaker link? Like I'm more vulnerable than the others because of my mom?"

Mother doesn't respond at first.

"Ig?" Miles says, sounding more than a little pissed. "If you jeopardize this mission, I swear to Christ, I'll—"

Mother drowns him out, her voice in Ig's head loud and malevolent, seething. "I chose you because of your connection to the land and seas, *child*. You, above all, have that extraordinary sense. I will not be denied what I wish." There's a short pause. Then, "I have no choice now."

Ig blinks, gaze shifting to the gathering monsters.

She draws in a breath to warn the others.

But it's too late.

Far too late.

Mother's offspring surge over Ig and Verity. All teeth and ravenous darkness. Verity manages one shot before something like a *Dunkleosteus* crossed with a *Liopleurodon* chomps her in two. Blood clouds the water. The legs of her mech kick sporadically.

Someone screams through the speakers just as a cavernous mouth snaps shut over her.

All the red lights flicker. A warbly alarm blares. A faint voice repeats, "Pressure warning. Pressure warning."

She has just enough time to draw in a shaky breath when a sharp tooth plunges through the nanoglass of the hatch and—

Ig blinks.

The monsters are still hovering behind Mother.

It was a…what? Dream? Vision?

"Ig? *Ig*? What the hell is going on with you?" Verity moves into her view. Ig can't see her face through the visor but imagines the biggest frown.

"That is what will happen," Mother whispers, "if you do not obey my wishes and leave. The odds are not in your favor, Ignia."

"Guys," Ig says. "We need to go. Right now."

"*What?*" Miles shouts, hurting Ig's ears. "We can't—"

"Look at them," Ig shouts back, fire raging within. "Fucking *look* at them! All Mother has to do is give the signal and we're all dead."

"So, let her," Ash says. "Let them get close. I highly doubt they can catch us at full speed."

He has a point, and yet…

"She can hear us..." Ig murmurs.

"Huh?" Verity says. "What do you mean?"

"Mother," Ig says. "She can hear us. She knows everything we're planning." Her gaze lifts. At first, there's nothing but murk, then she sees them. More offspring gliding above Mother.

Below, it's too dark to see, but she can imagine all the monsters down there too.

Heart thudding, she says, "They're above and below us too."

"Goddamn it," Miles growls. "We—"

"Retreat," Bracken says. "We got what we came for. Let...her be."

Everyone falls quiet, until...

"No," Miles says. "Mother is messing with you all. Look at the offspring, then squint. They're not really there."

Ig tries this. The monsters remain. She manages a couple breaths and says, "That's her messing with *you*. Does everyone else see them?"

A slight pause, and both Verity and Ash say, "Yes."

"Time...to go," Bracken says.

"Like *hell*," Miles booms. "They're not really there! She's gotten to all of you. Listen, I know what it's like to be controlled by things like this. We—"

"I can...and will...shut your mech...down," Bracken says. "It's time to go. We...were wrong...to interfere with nature."

A ding and Ig's mech says, "Incoming private message: "This...is Bracken. This message...is for...all of you. If Mother can...hear us, it's...through the open link between mechs. The...offspring are close enough. Leave her...and I will...blow her up."

Ig's heart trip-hammers. But, what if that's the wrong move too? What if Mother is lying or creating some weird delusional manifestation? What if this isn't really happening and they're all still on the sub?

Madness, it seems, is undetectable.

What's the truth? What's the lie? Is everything a lie? Is it all truth?

With a creature that can get into the heads of its prey, this scares Ig more than anything.

What if they're already dead and stuck in this Purgatory and meant to battle Mother for all of eternity?

Ig shivers while it all twists through her mind like thorny brambles.

Or, maybe, Mother is influencing her thoughts.

Or...maybe it's all true and, like any living thing...Mother wants to live. She wants her children to live. Is it wrong to deny life?

"Let her be," Bracken says. "Time...to go."

"Goddamn it," Miles says. After a couple heart beats, he adds. "Okay. Ig's plan has been compromised. Fall back."

She doesn't know who compromised what, but perhaps it's for the best. Besides, the sooner she can get to the mainland and to her mom, the better.

She just hopes Murdock hasn't hurt her mom.

Yet…

"What about Anna and me?" Ig asks Mother. "You said if we leave, you'll give her back."

"Ig, what…?" Verity says, then stops.

"We are past that now," Mother says. "Be gone, child. Live your life full."

Anger flares in Ig. "You lying bitch. You said—"

"Ig," Bracken says, voice calm. "Let's go home."

She glares at Mother for a moment, then positions herself away. At her side, Verity does the same.

"Full forward thrust," Ig says and in less than a second, she jets through the water

At the sixty-meter mark, something lifts from her mind. A dark cloud evaporates. Thick fog lifts…

Ig blinks, and for the first time she realizes what kind of hold Mother had on her.

At seventy-five meters, she tells her mech to "mild thrust" and finally, "slow thrust." Bracken comes into view shortly after.

Once Verity, Miles, and Ash arrive, Bracken says, "Let's thank Mother…for allowing us to take samples…from her."

"Wait, what?" Miles says.

"Look at her," Bracken manages through the wheezing. "Marvel at her beauty."

As he speaks, the offspring encircle Mother.

"She is a queen," Bracken says.

"I don't…" Verity begins, stops.

"Just…for a second," Bracken says. "Let's honor her."

Before anyone can respond, Mother, along with the offspring surrounding her, become a deep crimson cloud. Tattered body parts billow toward Ig and her group, then casually drift toward the surface.

"We…need to go…now," Bracken said while everyone stops and stares.

With the mech enhancing everything, Ig watches the carnage. The torn-off jaws, the eyeballs, all the pieces of monsters. She's almost sure she spots a dark tentacle twitching among all the bits and pieces.

She can't lie to herself, either. Her heart sinks a bit.

Before her, a family has been destroyed.

"That's…not all…the offspring," Bracken manages. "We have to—
"

Something extremely large and dark glides in front of the crimson cloud, sweeping the floating mess away with its great tail.

Ig remembers only one offspring being so large.

The one that bit through the sub.

A true monster, if ever there is one. Mother, despite her size, doesn't compare to this thing's ferocity. Perhaps it's her eldest born. A creature not quite ready to leave its mother's presence. Or…like in a beehive, a soldier devoted to his queen. One ready to fight and kill every threat to the colony. One willing to die for her.

"Can we outrun it?" Verity asks.

A pause. Then Bracken says, "Not now."

"I think," Ash says. "If we rapid pulse right now, we'll—"

"No," Bracken says. "As large as that one is…we'll…only get so far."

Ash sighs. "You're right. One swish of its tail and it'd have us as soon as we get moving."

"So," Miles says. "What the hell are we going to do?"

Ig's gaze narrows on the monster as it circles back around, this time much closer. It takes at least two minutes for the creature to pass by completely. She draws in a breath and says, "We kill it."

Someone grunts, she's not sure who.

Silence sprawls out until Bracken says, "The eyes."

"Huh?" Miles sounds like he's on the verge of a breakdown.

"Aim…for its eyes."

"Like Jörmungandr," Miles mutters.

"Ex…actly. Most…vuln…erable spots."

"Okay," Ash says, "seriously, Bracken. Save your air. You're sounding—"

"Heads up," Verity shouts.

Ig barely gets her mech positioned right before they begin firing laser bursts at the monster's glowing, amber eyes. She fires a blue beam, slicing it back and forth across the creature's face as it descends upon them. Its toothy maw opens, obscuring the eyes, and she aims the beam directly into the back of its throat.

Bits of charred flesh float like chum.

"Move," Miles shouts.

They all do.

"Full right thrust," Ig says, though not fast enough.

The creature crashes down into the shelf of rock the group had been hovering over. The force, being so close to impact, tosses Ig. She tumbles through the dark waters. The side of her head slams into the inner-mech and…she knows no more…

CHAPTER 20

A sensation of flipping end over end. All is darkness.

The force of the impact driving her farther and farther away.

Or is it?

When the mech naturally stabilizes, Ig gradually wakes up to shouting.

"Get back, get back! Holy shit!"

"It's gonna crash down. Look out!"

"Rapid pulse!"

"Rapid pulse."

Two more "rapid pulse" commands.

Even in the sloshy stew of her mind, Ig knows she's just been left alone. They all jetted away. Only her and the monster now. Her entire mech quakes. Lights flicker. Alarms wail. All the monitors sputter, save for two, which are completely black.

I'm going to die now, she thinks, heart bashing against her ribs. Her chest and throat tighten but when she goes to use her inhaler, only a tiny puff of medicine comes out. It helps a little. At least the tightening sensation eases enough for her to think.

"H-Hello?" she calls out.

She waits, but no one answers.

The high-density lamps wink on and off, darkness swelling in. Darkness above. Darkness below. Even when the lamps are on, they barely break such a deep black. Like she's trapped in an obsidian box.

She tries another puff from the inhaler, getting yet another meager inhale of medicine.

The reserve canisters for her inhaler were on the sub.

She has a few more at home, but—

Something crashes into her, driving her deep into the Devil's Trench. So fast, the entire mech goes crazy once more with all the flickering lights and alarms. Then...

"Pressure warning. Pressure warning." Over and over. One of the monitors flashes red with white letters. WARNING—Dangerous level of external pressure detected.

The entire mech groans. Metal slowly buckling. The hatch's nanoglass cracks, refuses, cracks, refuses. The microscopic bots work hard to keep the glass from shattering.

On a smaller monitor, her depth reads: 4,320 feet. And that number is rising fast the deeper she plummets. And yet, no matter how she tries, she can't break free.

Something is forcing her deeper into the Devil's Trench. The only problem is...whatever has it, it's not carrying her with its mouth. A tentacle, perhaps? She can't see a damn thing other than some shiny, crocodile-like skin when the lamps wink on.

The pressure warning turns to a PRESSURE HAZARD at 5,000 feet. All in big white letters flashing on the monitor. HAZARD—Mechanical suit will begin to deteriorate if pressure is not decreased.

And still she keeps—

When it happens, the impact is so jarring, the back of her head cracks against something metal behind her. A loud squeal cuts through the alarms. The nanoglass cracks, and the bots are slower to fix it, resulting in a droplet of water falling on her cheek. Cold, bleak water of the deep.

She's on her back, staring at the crocodile-like skin of whatever is sitting on top of her.

Panic erupts through her. Flashes cold and hot pulses. Her stomach churns and she fights the hot bile burning the back of her throat until she can finally swallow it down. She glances around, looking for something, anything, that might help her get out of this. But...there's only the mech with its stupid blinking lights and endless alarms. The monitors, which are all dark except the Pressure Hazard one, are all worthless.

She's trapped under something huge.

The monster that attacked them? The massive creature protecting its queen?

Ig has no idea, but it's all her frantic mind latches onto.

It's not moving, whatever it is. Is it dead?

"Help," she cries. "Someone, help! I'm trapped at, um..." She glances at the depth. "Five-thousand-six feet. Something is pinning me down. Please, if you can hear me...help!"

She waits a full ten minutes. Nothing. They really did abandon her.

Through the speakers that detect external sounds, something growls. And not just a small growl, either. A rumbling like rolls of thunder on a humid summer evening. A gathering storm.

Ig's breathing pauses, listening.

No one knows what other things lurk in the fathoms of the Devil's Trench. Though some have speculated real demonic titans stalk the dark depths, others claim nothing at all can live that deep. But maybe things can at this depth? It's deep, but nothing like what Ash claimed, which, according him, is immeasurable. And...

Is it getting harder to breathe? She draws in a breath and, yes...she has to pull in more than before. And it's not her asthma this time.

The thunderous growl shudders through the speakers, sounding much closer now. A long, bubbly hiss follows this. After...utter silence.

There is nothing in the universe which does not want to eat you. Who told her that? Grandpa? Mom? She can't remember. Or maybe it's the Great Spirit speaking to her now? Whichever the case, it's frightening. It gives the feeling that nowhere is safe and everything, even humans, want you dead. A scary thought, honestly.

And how is one supposed to overcome such fear? How does one glare into the eye of a thing that should not be and scream into its horrid face, I WILL NOT DIE?

"I will not die," she whispers.

She can move her right arm freely, but the left...it's pinned down. The left has the laser cannon. Shit...

"I will not die," Ig says, louder, and twists the mech's left arm. "I will *not* die," she shouts, giving the arm a yank.

Debris from the ocean clouds her vision.

As she waits for it to settle, she repeats, "I will not die."

The external growl rumbles through the speakers. Very close now.

Once the cloud of ocean silt settles, she finds her left arm mostly free. Or, rather, easier to move. If the thing pinning her down is dead or dying, there's only one way to get free.

"Laser," she says, lifting her left arm as much as possible.

The blue beam slices through the monster's reptilian skin and...

Blood. Her sight floods with crimson. Pink laced in red, organs spill onto her, entombing her in its guts. She roars, left arm lifting and slashing, laser cutting through everything it touches until finally she can sit up. Another minute, and she stands inside the beast.

It's gross, and some green liquid sprays from a pink sack. It mixes with the blood, creating a deep brown like early diarrhea. She nearly vomits again at the sight.

"Full upward thrust," she shouts, slashing the laser back and forth.

In about three minutes, Ig burst out of the creature, shooting upward in a trail of gore.

"Mild thrust," she says, because...curiosity. "Slow thrust." The mech slows. She can breathe freely again and realizes the water oxygen intakes might've been clogged earlier. The alarms still blare, and the warnings still scrawl across the one monitor, but some of the lights stop flickering.

"Stop," she says and positions the mech to look down.

It takes a moment for her brain to register what her eyes are seeing. Even then...it's nearly unbelievable.

Split in half, it is, indeed, the monster that attacked them all as Mother's soldier. And it's massive! Maybe two football fields long, maybe more. And just as wide as one. But this isn't all she notices. The halved creature rests upon a large stone shelf. Below is nothing but the deepest darkness.

So, she hadn't been pinned to the bottom of the Devil's Trench. Ash was right. Its depth must be...

It rears out of the darkness. Something twice as large as the thing she just cut through. A monster, from what she can tell, resembles a scorpion and a squid. Its long pincers extend over the other monster's corpse. Large mandibles snap. It's so unlike any of Mother's offspring, it gives her pause. Perhaps...this thing isn't from Mother at all...

If so, where is it from? Has it always lived in the Devil's Trench? Or, like some say, is it some kind of demonic fallout? A creature spliced with an Earthly thing like a lobster and a demon?

This...she doesn't know and there's no evidence to really judge. But, if she's to accept it, the demonic angle bodes well enough. Considering Mother shouldn't even exist. Unless...shit...unless Mother is a demonic splice too...

In her culture, there aren't demonic forces, but rather bad and evil spirits. Because, darkness must always balance out the light and vice versa. The Wendigo first comes to mind as a malevolent spirt. A darkness which preys on people. Dark spirits stalk the earth, so why not the sea too? Makes sense.

The monster clamps half of the dead creature with a pincer and pulls it into its eager mandibles where the tail and stomach (guts and all) are quickly consumed. Practically slurped down like spaghetti. Its other pincer snaps down on the upper part of the dead creature.

Enough.

"Full upward thrust," she says and shoots out of the deepest known part of the Devil's Trench.

When she's around one thousand feet from the surface, she works her way down from mild thrust to full stop. Barely above the trench, she hovers and glances around.

The vast space Mother had taken up is gone. Now there's only the open ocean and whatever other mysteries it hides. Scattered and floating are the remains of Mother and her nearby offspring. So many more offspring might be lurking. It's hard to tell.

"Hello?" she calls, not really expecting an answer.

She turns away from the floating debris of Mother's tattered flesh. A fog she didn't know she had slithers out her mind and she can think clearly again.

That's Mother's hold leaving me, she realizes.

She exhales a long, slow breath. Even her lungs feel better. Not tight or on the verge, just…normal.

"Hello?" she calls. "Anyone out there? Team Two? Bracken? Verity? Miles? Ash?"

All the monitors in the mech are aglow and giving her a three-sixty view around her. The sensors are silent. The ocean is just as silent and still.

No one answers her call.

The ocean, to most sailors, is a lonely place. But below the surface, with all the darkness and quiet…it's much worse. It's like floating in a void. A forgotten oblivion.

She sighs. "Full forward thrust." The mech jets forward and she positions it so she's shooting like a large bullet through all the murk.

Before long, the Devil's Trench is nothing but a bad, horrible memory.

CHAPTER 21

Miles away from the Devil's Trench, with no communication, nor sensing the second team who were supposed to clean up Mother's remains, Ig begins to wonder if something went horribly wrong while she was trapped under the dead monster.

Did Murdock send another—?

Her answer is quickly revealed as she shoots by a silvery sub.

"Mild thrust." She waits for the mech to slow, turning to face the sub as she does. "Slow thrust." She lets the mech slow to a crawl. "Full stop."

The sub isn't very large and it's just floating there. Maybe fifty yards away.

She slow thrusts, inching closer and trying to pick out a logo, or anything that might identify the sub.

Crackling static fills the speakers and...

"We have a lock on you, mech. Cease your momentum and state your name."

The voice is male and ugly sounding. She can almost imagine a husky white guy with a bristly beard munching on a bratwurst or something. Drinking a beer, probably. Regardless, the man has a fairly good vocabulary to make such a command.

She's almost tempted to full thrust away from the sub and try to lose them, but—

"Ig? Ig, is that you?"

She manages a breath. "Verity?" Ig checks the monitors, but doesn't see anything, except for the sub.

"We thought you were dead," Verity says. "Coming to find you."

"Where are you?"

A soft chuckle. "You're looking at us, hun."

Relief spills through her. "The sub? Shit, I thought it might've been one of Murdock's—"

A loud clank and the mech blares, "Pressure warning. Pressure warning."

"Oh my God," Verity shouts.

Through one of the monitors, she catches sight of snapping mandibles and a chill scuttles over her skin. The thing from the deeper part of the Devil's Trench? But how? There's no way it's so fast to follow her.

Unless there's more than one...

"It's like a scorpion with tentacles," Verity says.

"Ig," Miles says. "It has you in one of its pincers. If you can move your left arm back, you might be able to shoot laser bursts right in its ugly-ass face."

Everything quakes.

Heart hammering, she manages to dislodge her left arm and point it as far back as it will go.

"Fire," Miles shouts.

"Laser burst," Ig cries.

In the monitor with the mandibles, she watches six blue bursts slam into its mangled face. Something between a carp, shark, and lobster. A conglomeration of all. Ugly, indeed. The amber eyes appear to widen with each blast until eventually…

The pressure warning stops.

"It let you go," Miles says. "Cut that bastard in half!"

Ig spins the mech and faces the monster. Yes, the very same that ate the dead creature, which nearly crushed her to death about half an hour ago. Hundreds of grey tentacles writhe where its legs should be. Although, they appear to be more about swimming than grasping. They whip and toil, though none strike out at her as with Mother.

She gives it no time to react and shoots a solid laser beam into its right eye. It bursts, the eye. Though, with the eyes being on stalks, it's only half blind. Nothing enters the brain. It shoots out a pincer, and she scoots away before it can clamp down on her again. Ig roars, slicing the blue laser beam across the ugly face again and again until focusing her efforts directly between its elongated eyes.

Black, smoky bubbles froth the water until finally the creature falls limp and sinks, tentacles quivering while it slowly falls toward the ocean floor.

Loving the Earth and Sea? She feels like a traitor to both. But, in a world where things will eat you if given a chance, she must fight back.

Mom's life depends on her.

She finds the port of entry to the sub and eventually let in. As soon as there's an All Clear, she opens the hatch to her mech and crawls out. Being practically gravity free the entire time, she collapses on the landing just beyond the mech.

Verity and Ash help Ig to her feet and place her on a nearby metal bench. It takes her a long moment to orientate herself.

Verity hunkers down in front of her, face plastered in worry. "Are you okay? Does anything hurt?"

"No," Ig says. "Just feel weird."

"Lack of gravity," Ash says. "You'll come around in a couple minutes."

She knows this already but favors him with a smile and nod anyway.

"We don't have time to go back and clean up Mother's remains," Bracken says, sidling up beside Ash. "No need to anyway, since our second team here destroyed Murdock's fallback sub."

"They didn't see it coming," Verity says, though her face is solemn.

Lost lives are lost lives, regardless of which side they cling to.

"We're turning around," Bracken says. "We have a meeting with Murdock we can't miss, after all."

While her mech is being secured by robots, Ig frowns at Bracken. "How long has it been since Murdock called us?"

Bracken lowers his head in apparent thought. "About three hours. I think."

Ig's heart whip-cracks. "We need to hurry."

He nods. "We needed to get you secured first."

A thought fights its way to the surface. "Why did you all leave me like that?"

Verity gives a long sigh and gazes into Ig's eyes. "It wasn't like that. We thought it ate you. We didn't find any lifeforms, other than the other things in the deeper trench."

Ig nods, not sure what to say.

Bracken clears his throat and says, "Let's get you buckled in. We're going to hyper speed to the mainland. Be there in less than an hour."

"With even that," Ash says, "we should meet Murdock's deadline of five hours."

"If he hasn't already killed her," Ig mutters.

"Hey." Verity smacks Ig's leg. "Stay positive, okay?"

"Easy for any of you to say," Ig says. "It's not your mom, right? Stay positive?" She really doesn't mean to hurt anyone, but… "Sorry if it's a little hard for me to stay fucking positive here."

Verity glances at Ash. Ash sighs and walks away.

Bracken huffs out a breath. "Okay. Follow me. You need to get buckled in before we go into hyperdrive."

She manages to stand on her own, albeit a tad wobbly. Still, knees quivering, Ig follows Bracken out of the loading bay, or whatever it's called on this sub since it's much different than the other one. Larger, for one. The next room, as they step through a wide doorway, boasts a couple rows of high-backed seats with harnesses, and a few hyper-pods. To the right, like the other sub, is a short stairway to what she assumes is where all the shooting is done.

"I thought we needed to clean up Mother's remains?" Ig asks while Bracken motions for her to take a seat.

"There's no real need now that his second team is gone. What matters now is your meeting with Murdock. We need to hurry."

"Why?" Ig says, buckling into the harness.

Bracken pauses in mid-turn. His head lowers. Half turned away, he says, "Why, what?"

"Why are you tossing all caution to the wind to help me?"

He grunts, head still lowered. "Maybe…because I owe you for risking your life and the samples. Maybe I'm making up for all the wrong I've done in my life. Losing my wife and daughter because of my own, stupid stubbornness." He sighs. "But I think it's more you and your mother deserve to live a full, natural life. This is what the Resistance is about." He finishes, turning away and walking back to the docking bay.

Ig watches him go, mouth opening and closing, not sure what to say. Tears tingle her eyes and slip down her cheeks.

The world has shown her or her tribe little respect and a lot less love. Indeed, the world has been a bastard. A thorny, wretched struggle every day.

But this…what Bracken said…this gives her hope.

And, sometimes, hope is all there is to keep you alive.

CHAPTER 22

"Mainland in ten minutes," Miles says through the speakers.

Verity nudges Ig. "You ready for this?"

"Don't think I have a choice."

On Ig's right, Verity snorts. "We always have a choice, but it's more about what's right or wrong. You made the *right* choice."

"Clever," Ig says, shooting Verity a smile. She places a hand over Verity's. Their eyes meet and Ig's heart flutters. "Thank you."

Verity frowns. "For what? *You* saved *me*."

Ig chuckles and squeezes Verity's hand. "Or we saved each other."

The frown on Verity deepens before lifting and the woman beams a bright smile at Ig. She claps her other hand Ig's. "Maybe we have."

"Murdock might have people ready for us to dock," Bracken says. "So, we'll hang back and monitor the land before surfacing fully."

"What's the plan?" Ig asks.

He winks. "Those mechs work just as well on land."

Ig doesn't get it at first, then all the gears catch in her mind. "We're using the mechs to overpower him."

"Correct," Bracken says. "I will also be calling in a few reserves."

"You think he's that well-guarded?" Ig asks.

"Oh," Bracken says. "He is. Even when you can't see those guards, he has protection at all times."

"Lovely."

He smiles from across the aisle. "He doesn't know we're coming. That will be our advantage."

Ig nods, turning all the possible scenarios over in her head. So many things could go wrong but might also go very right.

Her mind drifts to Mom. How is she doing? Are they taking care of her?

Or is it all a trap and she's already dead?

She draws in a breath and blows it out slowly.

Time to end this…

***

"All clear," Miles says. "No lifeforms at the docks or within one hundred yards."

"Here we go," Bracken says. "As soon as we dock, everyone get suited up in their mechs."

Beside him, Ash nods. "And our backup?"

"Once we dock and suited up," Bracken says, "I'll put out the call."

Ash nods again.

"Prepare to surface," Miles says.

Minutes pass, then Miles says, "Docking. Better get dressed, kids."

Bracken and Ash unbuckle their harnesses. Ig follows suit, along with Verity.

Hurrying toward the docking bay, Ig asks, "What about Miles?"

Ash shoots her a smile. "Every side needs a wild card."

Before she can ask him what he means, Ash lies down in his sleek, blue mech. It closes around him, sealing airtight. Bracken and Verity get into their own mechs.

Ig's still rests in the loading area.

She opens the hatch and climbs in. Once the hatch is shut, the mech comes to life around her. Only takes a couple seconds to go online. Once it's running, she orders it to stand. The largest of them, she towers over Bracken, Verity, and Ash.

"This way," Bracken says through the speakers and one of the blue mechs walks to the back of the room.

Before long, they get on a large elevator. The ceiling opens and all four of them emerge into fresh air. Not that they can really breathe it in, but it's nice to finally see the sky. They leap from the sub to the steel docks, Bracken leading the way.

"I'm going to send a message to the base," Bracken says. "This mech has a direct link. Anyway. Standby until I receive word."

"How much time do we have?" Ig asks.

"About one hour before we're late," Ash says. "So, Bracken, make it quick."

"It's an urgent response," Bracken says. "Should be informed in a minute. Maybe less."

"In a half-hour," Ash says, "we'll need to move."

So…as much as Ig wants to storm home, she must wait. And while the minutes tick by without a word from Bracken, she soon grows impatient and sneaks away from the small group. Too much time has already been wasted.

Ig sets out alone toward home.

Enough is enough.

It's not until she's about a mile away when Verity says through the speakers, "Ig? Where'd you go?"

Enough is enough, and Ig decides not to answer Verity.

"Shit, guys, I think she…"

Perhaps, all along, this is something she must face for herself. On her own. Face to face with the real monster. The man who has destroyed so many lives and threatens her own.

Closer and closer to home, she thinks, *Enough is enough…*

Come whatever may…this is the end.

CHAPTER 23

None of her sensors go off. Indeed, the entire area appears void of life, save for ground squirrels.

The sensors echo from the cabin, revealing zero life.

Ig's heart sinks, barely beating as she approaches her home.

Zero life is not a good sign. At all.

Ig approaches the cabin, readying the mech and trying to keep an eye on all the monitors at once. A task much harder than it sounds while stepping up to the front door. The mech is far too large to fit through the doorway. Regardless, she gives the door a knock and backs away.

The door does not open, nor do the sensors verify movement inside. It—

"Ms. Hawkins," a hideously familiar voice says. "So glad you made it on time."

She turns, finding not only Murdock, but at least eight dozen soldiers. Four of which are in mechs of their own.

"Where's my mom, asshole?" When Murdock frowns, she realizes she forgot to tap the external speaker option. She does, and repeats, "Where's my mom, asshole?"

Murdock, with his slicked-back black hair gleaming like a skintight cap on his head in the afternoon light, chuckles. He points at the cabin. "Why, inside, of course. Can't have her out here in all this polluted air, you know." He brings out a small comb and runs it through is his black mustache, then stows the comb back in the breast pocket of his white suit.

"I need to know if she's still alive."

One of his dark eyebrows lift. "And do you have the samples?"

"Yes."

"How am I supposed to know?"

She grits her teeth from shouting at the man and barely manages, "How am *I* supposed to know Mom is still alive?"

He stares at her for a while, grunts and straightens a bit. "Oh, you're a clever one." His grin lengthens. "I like that."

"I could care less what you like," Ig says. "I need proof Mom is okay, and you have the cure you promised. Then I'll—"

Murdoch shakes his head, waggling a manicured finger at her. "Oh, little Ignia, you forget who's making the rules here."

"Shut up," she bursts out. "You killed Anna!"

This stops him. The grins leaks from his face, revealing the old man he really is for a few seconds. Then his eyebrows knit together in a scowl. She has less than a second to regret what she said before he pulls a strange gun from his hip and fires a shit into the mech's chest. The force alone is enough to stagger the mech.

A dull ache pokes her stomach, a mild burn. When she looks, all the air whistles out of her. The bullet, or whatever it was, pushed the metal of the mech inward so far it thumped her stomach. A little stronger of a blast, and it would've ripped right through the metal and she'd be dead.

Murdock, gun still pointed at her, says in a low voice, "You ever speak her name again, so help me, I'll kill you and your mother right here and now." Finally, he blinks, glances back and forth, then holsters the gun. He runs a hand over his oiled hair, visibly shuddering. "Let's make this clean, Ignia. I know my daughter and you...had a fling, but—"

"We loved each other!"

A shadow passes over his face and his hand falls to the butt of the gun again. The hand curls into a shaky fist. "Where are the samples?"

"Where is my mom?"

"In the goddamn..." Murdock takes a breath. "In the cabin, as I have said. Now, let's get this over with, shall we?" Form his pants pocket, he brings out a vile of green liquid and shakes it. "Your mother is waiting."

Without Mother's influence, Ig smiles. "Is that the real cure?"

He actually spits at her this. "Of course it's the *fucking* cure."

Ig's gaze drifts back and forth, calculating all the men and the four mechs. She'll need to be quick and move around a lot to kill most of them. The only trouble will be the other mechs. If they surround her...

Maybe she should've waited for Bracken and the others after all.

Once more, Murdock regains his composure. From what she could remember, he always appeared so proper, patient, and polite, even while insulting someone. Now, however, something has changed. He's unpredictable. Unhinged. Things that might not have set him off now does.

Maybe it's best to tread lightly now.

At least until she can figure out a plan where she doesn't die. Which appears grim right now. Too grim.

"Fine," Ig says. "What do you want me to do?"

A smug smile lurches over her lips. "Get out of that thing, and I'll hand you the cure. You're free to go save your mother." The smile softens into something almost genuine. "I give you my word."

She snorts. "Your word..."

"Yes," Murdock says, smile dissolving. "Despite what you think, I am not a monster." A soldier hands him a tablet. He taps something and turns the screen to her.

Ig's heart aches the moment Anna's smiling face comes into view. Playing out on the tablet's screen is something Anna never before mentioned. It's of her and Murdock building a snowman. Not in this region, obviously, but one further south. Florida, perhaps. It's beautiful, picturesque. Anna is maybe ten years old. Both of them are laughing as they roll the balls of snow to create a tall snowman. They finish with a top hat and a carrot for a nose. "I love you, Daddy," Anna says as Murdock scoops her into his arms. He kisses her rosy cheek. "Love you too, sweet girl."

The video ends, giving way to another. This one, Anna is a little older. Thirteen, maybe? Regardless, she's all smiles while she and her dad build birdhouses. The next video, she's about the age when Ig met her. When they first became friends. Fifteen, or so. It's of her and Murdock on floats in a pool while a familiar tune plays in the background. Something popular during that time. Ig knows it, though can't quite remember the singer or band. The beat, though...the melody...

Anna and Murdock are laughing and trying to eat nachos from a floaty resembling a donut. This brings a smile to Ig's face. Despite Murdock being there, seeing Anna laugh and smile fills her heart. It's been so long since she's heard that smile worthy laugh and brilliant smile. And it all ended so quickly.

The videos end and Murdock hands the tablet to a nearby soldier, who then hands it off to someone else.

He fetches a heavy sigh. "So, you see...you are not the only one who loved her. Not a day goes by when I don't watch those videos and weep, or smile." He steps forward, stops. "She was my heart. My soul." His gaze drifts away from Ig. "But she won't be gone for much longer."

"What?" A deeper frown shadows Ig's face.

Murdock shakes his head. "Never mind. Get out of that thing. Take the cure and live a happy life with your mother." His voice softens a bit. "Before you know it...they won't be there to laugh with anymore."

Yes, Murdock has changed. The sense of something off with the man strengthens in Ig. Or, perhaps, he truly is just a grieving father. The videos proved they shared some good times together, and yet...what about all the things Anna said about him? The bad things. The abusive things. The nefarious actions and plots.

Had Anna been lying? If so, why would she do that? To what point?

To Ig, it feels like Anna was trying to warn her about Murdock. Only, Ig didn't heed the warnings and the man injected Mom with those ancient parasites.

Anna was trying to warn me...

"So," Murdock says, voice booming. "What is it going to be, Ms. Hawkins? You get out of that mech and save your mom, or I shoot through that nanoglass and obliterate your head?"

"Well," Ig says, "since you asked so nicely."

Murdock draws his gun. "Do *not* fuck with me right now, Ignia."

Her heart stutters, and she reaches to open the hatch.

A blue beam slices through all four of the mechs and half the soldiers. Bodies fall, some cut in half, other in angled pieces. One man, who didn't die in his mech, crawls out holding his guts in his hands, screaming. Blood bubbles out his gaping mouth. Before long, he stumbles and falls flat on his face.

"What—?" Murdock manages just as one of the sleek, blue mechs land between him and Ig.

"Get back, Ig," Bracken says.

Heart slamming, she gets the mech to walk backward and away from the blue mech and Murdock.

"It's over, Murdock," Bracken says, and Ig finally realizes it's him who stands between her and Murdock.

"Well, hello, Mr. Tull." A loud bang sounds. "And good-bye."

The blue mech in front of her staggers, drops to its knees. Through the speakers, Ig listens to Bracken grunting in pain.

The gun! Murdock shot Bracken with that damn gun.

"Laser," she says, hatred frothing, and starts forward.

Murdock isn't there anymore.

"Where…?"

"Ran off," Bracken says, coughs. "Coward."

Ig steps close to Bracken as his mech visibly shudders. A large hole smolders in his mech's chest.

"Oh no," she mutters.

With a weak chuckle, Bracken says. "Not as bad as it looks."

The rest of whatever soldiers were left alive depart, running through the tall grasses, presumably following their frightened boss. Not real soldiers, but hired guns is Ig's guess. Tamed mercenaries, even.

Sunset splashes the land in a scarlet and gold. Won't be long before night eats the day.

"Holy shit," Miles says as he storms over in his mech. "What the hell happened?"

"Apparently," Bracken says, "Murdock figured out how to make mech-piercing bullets."

Miles kneels, large mech fingers inspecting the smoldering hole in Bracken's chest. "Tell me it missed you."

"I could," Bracken says, "but I'd be lying. The mech slowed the momentum of the bullet down, but, yeah…I'm hurt pretty bad in here."

"How hurt?" Ash asks as he and his mech make their way over.

"Bleeding," Bracken says.

"We need to get you inside then," Ash says. "Might be able to stop the bleeding."

"No," Bracken nearly shouts. "Get Murdock. He needs to be stopped."

"We're not leaving you to die," Ash says.

"Yes. You are. Get moving."

"If Murdock gets away," Miles says, then sighs, "all of this was for nothing, really. Well, except for saving Ig's mom, and millions with the samples, of course."

Ig hardly registers this. She straightens the mech, watching the wannabe soldiers flee. How far away is Murdock now?

"Oh, hell," Verity says as she steps beside Ig. Her mech is a good two feet shorter. Still at least three feet above even a six-foot man or woman, though.

"You…don't have much time," Bracken says, sounding much weaker.

"You guys go get Murdock," Ash says. "I'll stay with Bracken."

"Like hell you will," Bracken says. "I'll be fine. Stop that asshole."

"Incoming group private message from Ash Barrington: "You three go. I'll take care of him."

Without a word, Ig, Miles, and Verity shoot forward at a speed faster than any vehicle on earth. Ig has no idea how fast, but fast enough to catch up to the wannabe soldiers in less than a minute. Miles takes them all out with a single laser swipe.

There's no sign of Murdock.

"No way he can run that fast," Verity says.

Ig's gaze floats over the tall grasses until she spots something odd. An even part in the grasses, like it's been combed. She lifts and arm at the part. "There."

It takes Miles and Verity a moment.

"He has some kind of vehicle," Miles says, pointing out the obvious.

"Let's go," Ig says and leads the way through the path in the grass.

The path veers west until they run out of the tall grasses and into mild sand dunes.

"Shit," Verity says.

Ig scours the dunes until she comes across a strange feathered pattern. Following the feathered path through the sand, she tries to ignore the poke of metal at her stomach where Murdock's bullet hit. Another foot closer and she'd be dead. This, she firmly believes in, considering how easily Murdock's shot made it through Bracken's mech. Though not as bulky, she assumes those mechs are strong too. An upgrade to what she's in now. Or, is she in the upgrade?

She's not so sure.

In less than ten minutes, Ig catches up to Murdock. He's on a hovercycle. One of the fastest known bikes in existence, though not fast enough for a mech, apparently.

Ig, rage reheating, blasts by Murdock. She catches a brief, shocked reaction, then cuts in front of him.

The result is devastating…for Murdock. His hovercycle crashes into Ig's mech and he's thrown into her hard enough for blood to splatter the hatch's nanoglass. She lets him fall to the sandy ground where he lies. Not moving.

"Well," Verity says as she eases to a stop opposite of Ig. "That's one way to stop him. Good job, hun."

Ig smiles, though most of her focus is on Murdock's lifeless body. "Is he dead?"

Miles approaches and places a large mech finger on Murdock's throat. A couple seconds, and he says, "He's still alive. Might have a concussion."

"Poor guy," Verity says, mock sniffling.

"So," Ig says, "what now?"

"Take him back to Bracken, is my guess," Miles says.

Ig lowers the mech and scoops Murdock's unconscious body up into her arms. She's about to turn when he says, "Goodbye, Ignia."

The gun blast comes directly after the sharp pain in her head.

Then she knows nothing.

CHAPTER 24

"…up!"

Everything is a murky pond, rippling outward. She surfaces, dips under.

"…wake up, Ig!"

The voice is familiar, and it only takes a moment for all the gears in Ig's mind to click into place. She emerges from the murk of her mind and instantly rejects it. A sharp pain cuts through the side of her head. Something is beeping, driving the pain deeper like a blunt spike.

"She's okay," Miles says. "Ig? I need you to open your eyes for me."

She groans at the swelling agony in her head and opens her eyes. Thankfully, it's dusk, and the light isn't torture on her eyes. The nanoglass of her mech is broken, though, very slowly, fusing itself together again.

"Wha…What happened?"

Verity and Miles, outside their mech and peering through the large hole in the nanoglass at her, glance at each other, then back at Ig.

"He shot you," Verity says. "You don't remember?"

Ig shifts her weight, winces at the sharp pain running along the side of her head. When she touches the source of the pain, her fingers come back bloody.

She gasps. Her sight snaps to Verity and Miles. "What? He…he shot me? He—"

"Hey," Miles says, reaching in and patting her shoulder. "It's okay. *You're* okay. The bullet only grazed you."

Heart a frantic mess, she shakes her head, which sends tendrils of pain through her. "*Only* grazed me? It hurts like hell."

Miles smiles a bit. "Just a flesh wound. No stitches required. I think the blast hurt you more than the bullet. Knocked you out."

She sighed. "Where's Murdock?"

"Gone," Verity says. "Miles thinks he knows where he went, though."

"Only one place for a coward like that to go," Miles says. "He went home."

"And…" Ig sucks in a sharp breath while the pain stabs at her again. "And he probably has a small army protecting him right now."

"Probably," Miles says. He grins. "Wouldn't be any fun if he didn't." He pulls his arm out and taps the existing nanoglass. "This should fuse just fine. While it does, let's make our way to that bastard's home. I'm guessing you might know the way?"

Ig manages to get the mech upright. The shattered glass inside the mech scuttles like glittery spiders over her to the open hole in the hatch. As she gathers herself and tries to ignore the pain, the large, ragged hole closes. Completely fusing together. The tiny bots make a slight buzzing sound and an iridescent ripple flows over the hatch. Then all is clear.

If she'd been in the ocean, though, she'd already have drowned.

Nanoglass is great for small cracks, but when something actually penetrates...

"Ig," Miles says through the speakers. "I want you to hang back and let us take care of the heavy assaults. You're carrying the samples and we can't jeopardize those. We move a lot faster and can cut them down quickly."

She shrugs, even though he can't see it. "Okay."

They race across a small desert until they come to a small town. From there, they pause at a crossroads.

"Right," Ig says, remembering her sleepovers at Anna's house a little over six years ago.

They turn right and speed down a long, dusty road. Faster than in water, Ig's mech feels like a bullet destined for the real target.

But, can she really kill him when it comes down to it? Taking a life, of any kind, is a deep burden. Even now, Mother's death holds sway over her. But Murdock has committed so many crimes over the years, would the world really miss him?

Once upon a time, Murdock might have been a good person. If so, that was long ago and now...

Murdock's compound, not a home really, if Ig remembers correctly.

Every time she stayed over, Anna's massive house always felt like Ig was being trapped in a massive box. Indeed, Murdock and Anna lived in a mansion. Albeit a very fortified and guarded one.

"We need a better plan," Ig spouts, still trying to ignore the cut along the side of her head. The bullet itself is embedded in the back of mech, thankfully missing anything vital like hydraulic lines or wires.

"Like what?" Miles asks.

"We know he'll be heavily guarded," Ig says. "That place is a fortress. We need to sneak in if we're going to make it. Going in and trying to cut them all down is pretty much suicide."

Miles falls silent for the longest time. They all slow their pace until finally they stand in the middle of the road. Murdock's place isn't far now. About three miles, if she remembers right. Another few feet and she wouldn't be surprised if hidden sensors or satellites or something alerts Murdock to their presence.

If that hasn't happened already, of course.

"You're right," Miles says through her mech's speakers. "We need a better plan. Do you know of a secret way in?"

"No…" Ig trails off while her mind flips to a certain memory. One she hasn't really dwelled on for years.

They were both about fourteen and it was Ig's second time staying the night at Anna's place. Murdock hurried off to address some matter or another in his chambers, leaving Anna and Ig alone in the theater room. A massive room dominated by a huge screen, just like in a real movie theater. The room also had a pool table and a couple game consoles hooked to big screen TVs. There was a popcorn machine and a small stand with various candies. Anna and Ig hung out a lot in the theater room, playing video games and munching on popcorn and candy. And, oh, how they'd laugh. Their budding friendship grew into a beautiful flower in less than a year. It was also when Ig first began thinking of Anna as more than just a friend. More than a sister…

That night, though, was special. They were totally alone for the first time while Murdock attended to whatever nefarious thing that demanded his attention. And, for the first time, Anna led Ig by the hand out of the theater room to the main corridor. The corridor always gave Ig the sense of walking through a marble tunnel deep in the ground. Wide, its ceiling domed, the corridor was indeed made of marble, but not at all underground. Still, it always gave her that odd sense of adventure. As Anna pulled her along, she imagined herself a world-renowned explorer in search of some ancient artifact deep under a mountain where anything could pop out and try to kill her.

Laughing, Ig asked Anna where they were going. Anna shot a smile over her shoulder, though the only sound that came out was a silly giggle. Ig laughed and followed along. Her best guess fell on raiding the kitchen. Sometimes they could sneak out some good food, other than relying on candy and popcorn. And since the chefs went to their dorms at seven, the kitchen was usually abandoned. Easy pickings.

And yet, when the time came to turn for the kitchen, they raced by. Ig frowned, once more lost. Anna wasn't one to be so spontaneous. Running up the white, marble corridor, Ig's second guess was the pool room. A full indoor pool with a hot tub and everything. Sometimes they jumped in and swam just for fun.

But…no. They passed the way to the pool room, leaving Ig more than confused. Worried, Ig asked Anna again where they were going. And, as before, Anna gave her that over-the-shoulder smile and giggle.

Ig wasn't sure if she should laugh or yank her hand out of Anna's grip. Her grandfather used to say white people were strange creatures. Sometimes they turned on you like a rabid dog. Ig didn't believe it, nor did she think Anna would lead her to danger, but when something was spoken by an elder, it sunk its teeth in. She assumed it was like that for everyone, but then again, she didn't know.

Eventually, they found their way outside, dashing across the manicured lawn. The dew kissed Ig's bare feet while they ran behind the Jones' Mansion. The backyard, which was a vast expanse of hedge animals, Zen gardens, and an outdoor pool, was only lit by the full moon that night. Typically, there are outdoor lamps on.

When they reached the towering wall of the backyard, Anna spun to Ig and said, "I couldn't say anything in there, but I want to show you something."

Ig wanted to ask why she couldn't say anything inside the mansion, but before she could, Anna pulled her to a corner of the wall. A corner hidden behind pine trees and decorative shrubs.

"I found this a couple days ago," Anna said and pulled away a mass of stringy, green moss.

Ig peered into a large, black hole.

"I don't know what happened," Anna said, "but maybe the workers building it left an escape opening for us. Like, if there's a fire and we can only get out through the back."

"Does your dad know about it?" Ig asked.

"I don't know, but c'mon."

Anna tugged Ig into the dark crevasse. Everything echoed, even their breathing. Just like in a real tunnel. In a couple minutes, they emerged into a starry night. Anna whipped Ig around in a firm embrace. Ig's heart fluttered...

Ig sucks in a sharp breath now, shaking off the beautiful memory. "Backyard. There's an opening at the east corner."

"Big enough for us to fit through?" Verity asks.

"I don't know. I was fourteen when Anna showed it to me."

A slight pause. "You still love her, don't you?"

Ig's mouth opens, shuts, not sure how to respond. Because she loves Verity too. And, in a way, it feels like she might be cheating on Anna to really say so. Even if Anna is dead, it's hard to fully love Verity, no matter how strong the attraction is.

"Okay," Miles says, breaking the tension. "So, this opening, there's a chance we might fit through it?"

Ig manages a couple breaths, nods. "You two might. I don't know about me."

"Perfect," Miles says. "I need you to stay away from the firefight as much as possible anyway."

Ig glares at his mech, which stands front and center. "So, why am I even here?" Then she chuckles, void of humor. "Oh, that's right. You just need me to get inside. Got it."

"No," Miles says. "That's not why, and you know it. I need you to hang back because of the samples. But when shit hits the fan, your laser is stronger than ours and we might need you to do a sweep. You can scale the wall, I'm sure. If you can…stand on it and wait for my orders."

"Ig," Verity says. "Do you really think he has that much protection?"

"Oh, yes…especially now," Ig says.

"Are we killing him, or detaining?" Verity asks.

A long pause. "Detain," Miles says. "The bastard deserves to die, but we'll leave that up to Bracken and the others in the Resistance."

"He might be expecting us to sneak in from the back," Ig says. "Might be able to get in, pick him up, and get out without much trouble."

Miles grunts. "You said so yourself, he'll be heavily guarded now. There's gonna be trouble no matter which way we go in. But we might gain the upper hand sneaking in."

Another point resurfaces in Ig's mind. "He probably has drones, or sensors, or something to detect movement and all that. If so, we'll be swarmed by his guards."

"The mechs don't have cloaks, either," Miles mutters. "Shit."

No one says anything for about a full minute until Verity sighs. "So, what are we going to do? The longer we stand here, the better prepared he'll be."

"We take our chances," Miles says. "I doubt he's planning on just us coming. He'll be looking for a larger-scale attack. That's even if the coward is still there."

Ig turns in the direction of Murdock's compound. "He is."

"How do you know?" Verity asks.

"He has all he needs at his home. All the tech and manpower. He can dig in and wait until everyone kills themselves in a firefight. That's what he does. He plans and he sets the chess pieces and waits. He played us too."

"Yeah, well," Miles says, "I'm done playing. Let's go."

CHAPTER 25

If there are any sensors or anything, none of them get tripped as they move through a thick belt of woods to the back of Murdock's compound.

It ceased being a house or mansion the moment Anna died.

Most of the back wall is blanketed in green vines and while dusk is eaten by the night, those vines might as well be dark snakes shining under a half moon.

She pulls vines away, revealing the crevasse in the wall. Definitely too small for her mech, but Miles and Verity fit. Well, barely. It appears to be a tight fit, though they disappear within a few seconds.

Ig waits, feeling far too exposed and alone. And although the sensors and monitors pick up nothing, there's still this slippery sense of foreboding. Like an oily black spider in a bathroom stall. Silence stretches on for what feels like hours, but only really about a minute.

"We're in," Miles whispers. "No guards. The towers on top of the places appear deserted. Ig, can you climb the wall and spot us? We're going right to the back door."

"I'll try." Climb the wall? How the hell is she supposed to do that? It's one hundred feet tall, for shit sake.

"You mech should have a climbing feature," Miles says "Supposed to be used for underwater mountains, I think, but should work here."

Ig sighs. There isn't anything labeled climb, so she says, "Um, climb?"

The hands of the mech splay thick spikes literally sprout from the metal, covering the hands. A shudder rattles the mech, then, "Climb active."

In no time, she scales the wall all the way to the top. It's wide enough for ten of her mechs to stand on without toppling off. There are guard towers set about fifty meters apart, but the one nearest her is empty. A frown creases her face.

Something feels wrong.

She focuses her attention on Miles and Verity as they creep closer toward the back door. She watches them step around the pool and overgrown hedge animals. Apparently, Murdock hasn't thought to trim them in quite a while. The hedges only vaguely resemble animals. And the pool is void of water. Just a large, white hole in the ground. Sad, how he let everything go. Things Anna enjoyed, he now ignores.

Grief, she believes, tortures everyone differently.

That wrong feeling gnaws at the back of her mind like a ravenous rat. This is all too easy.

And yet, Miles and Verity arrive at the large backdoor of the compound and open it. Nothing. No alarms. Just…silence. Every light in the place appears to be off too. It's almost as if Murdock is planning…

Ig gasps. "An ambush."

"Wha—?" Miles begins, and the night explodes into bright light.

She's blinded for a moment and—

"Ah," Murdock's voice booms. "There you are, my friends! Was wondering if you would have the guts. For this, I applaud all of you. Even Ms. Hawkins up there on the wall. Sorry the bullet missed, dear heart. Maybe next time?"

Ig's vision adjusts to the abrupt light. She blinks, heart skipping a beat. Below are dozens of armed guards and what appears to be more than ten mechs. No one is on the wall with her, though. Which begs the question…what guns are pointed at her right now, and from where? Her gaze lifts to the towers on top of the compound. She can't tell if anyone is up there, though she assumes there is. With Murdock, anything is possible, or so she's learned.

On the ground, Verity and Miles are surrounded.

"Bastards," Miles says. "Ig, a little help?"

"I think he has guns on me too. From the towers."

"Probably. Move while you cut down as many of these assholes as possible. Focus on the mechs."

"Well," Ig says. "That makes me feel so much better. I have to dodge bullets now."

He chuckles. "It's like a game. Just try to be one step ahead."

"Easy for you to say, Mr. Former Seal."

He laughs and Ig scans the scene below her. The mechs aren't clustered together, but kind of dotted here and there among the guards. So, it's going to take more than just a swipe through the crowd.

"Any day now, Ig," Miles says.

She says, "Laser," draws in a breath, and tells the mech to side thrust while a blue laser beam slices through mechs and guards alike on the ground on the right. Concrete pieces burst in front of her. Oh, indeed there are guns on her. She dashes to the left and slices as many as she can until a bullet slams into her chest. High-caliber, leaving a small, dent, but not strong enough to pierce the mech. So, maybe, only Murdock has the mech-piercing bullets?

She slices through as many as she can, bullets catching her here and there, though leaving little damage. Only two mechs, save for Miles and

Verity, still stand. And what remains of Murdock's guards, they're fleeing in every direction.

Ig slices through the towers with her laser. The bullets stop flying from above. She's not sure if she killed them, but a break is a break. Below, the remaining mechs, three in all, and a handful of guards surge toward Miles and Verity from either flank.

She readies herself to take out as many as she can, but Miles and Verity do it for her, and much quicker. Within seconds, the mechs and guards are dead.

"Okay," Miles says. "Going in."

Ig watches them bash through the door and enter the compound, heart hammering. It doesn't take her long to scale down the wall and rush to the door.

She still has a score to settle after all...

***

The doorway is a bit small, but Ig chips away until she can squeeze through. She keeps forgetting how much larger her mech is compared to Miles' and Verity's. Soon enough, she finds herself standing in the very same massive corridor Anna led her through when she was fourteen.

Memories flood in. So many lovely memories of her dear Anna. She eventually shakes them off and clomps down the corridor. If all is the same, Murdock's chambers are a short hall before the theater room. Ig takes a chance and follows the hall to a dead end.

Here, she's stumped for a moment. Miles and Verity are nowhere to be seen, nor does she call to them. She wants to face this particular monster alone. Yet, maybe he redesigned the inside since she was last in it because she doesn't remember a dead-end wall.

"Fuck it," Ig says and sends a laser blast into the wall, not expecting much.

And yet...the wall itself wavers and sputters. It ripples and for but a moment reveals what really lies behind it.

A massive wooden door. Double doors, to be exact.

"Found you," Ig whispers and kicks the doors in.

The room beyond is massive, lit only by faux candles. A gloomy room dominated by a large aquarium. Ig bursts into Murdock's chambers. To the right of the aquarium is a full kitchen and bar. On the left, up a couple steps, is a huge wooden desk, intricately carved with what appear to be feathers.

Anna used to be obsessed with feathers.

Yes. Perhaps at one time, Murdock Jones wasn't the monster he is now.

Perhaps...

She scans the giant room, picking up nothing.

"Shit," she says under her breath, while moving deeper into the chambers.

He's not here, though. Maybe some other room? The vaulted basement? Or—

"I think about her every day, you know."

Ig's heart stutters. She stops the mech, searching for Murdock and still not finding him.

"I didn't kill her," he says, voice just above a whisper. "I know you and everyone thinks I did, but...that is something I could never do." A long sigh. "I have lived an extraordinary life, Ignia, but all the wonder and beauty died with her."

Ig moves forward. Slow, keeping her gaze shifting from the sensors and monitors, then through the hatch. Her chest is tightening, and she silently curses herself for not picking up a medicine canister from home before setting out. She works on regulating her breathing. In through the nose, out through the mouth. It worked before. Maybe it'll work now.

"I guess you could say everything I've done since her death was mostly for her. All this monster hunting and sample taking. I put too many people in harm's way knowing they might not make it out of the situation. Like Bracken and the Leviathan. I knew his team was a wrong fit to fix an oil rig. It wasn't the rig I wanted. It was a blood sample from the Leviathan. I put my trust in the lieutenant. Someone I should have given a psych test too before sending her out there with those innocent people."

Is she hearing him right? He almost sounds...sorry. Could be a trick, though.

Despite this, she says, "Why were you trying to get samples from sea monsters?"

"About the same reason why Bracken wants the plasma samples of the Mother of Monsters. To save lives." He pauses. Then, barely audible, "Or resurrect one."

"What are you talking about? Come out so we can talk."

"I'm in here, Ignia. The room directly in front of you. Don't worry, I won't shoot you again."

"Says the dude who shot me *twice*."

"I never claim to be above human impulses. I thought you were going to kill me. I do apologize. Come in. Please. Let's talk. Then, after that, if you still wish to kill me, I won't stop you."

As she approaches the doorway to the next room, her lungs loosen a bit.

The man stands in the smaller room, back to her, hands clasped behind him. He stares a blank wall. "The doorway is too small for you mech to fit through."

She snorts. "If you think I'm going to get out of it, you *are* insane."

He nods, though still doesn't turn to look at her. "Understandable. I have done little to earn your trust." He unclasps his hands and taps a small outcropping in front of the wall. "Six years. The longest of my life."

Six years since Anna died.

Ig nods. "Something we can agree on."

Murdock's head lowers. "I know she loved you too. As hard as it was for me to accept, I understand now."

"Do you?" A frown shadows her face.

"Yes. And your love for her is apparent, even now." He turns, finally facing her. "Ignia, we should not be fighting. We should be working together. For her." He reaches back, taps something, and the wall opens up behind him, revealing…

"I…what…is that…?" She gapes at the thing floating in a large tube of transparent fluid. She doesn't want him to answer though, because—

He smiles. One which appears genuine. "This is Anna."

Ig's gaze drifts over the brain and bobbing eyeballs, and down the spine with all its nerves. "This…no." She shakes her head "That—*why* would you do this?"

"I know she's hard to look at," Murdock says. "But it's her. Our Anna."

She shakes her head, fighting tears. "You're sick."

He fetches a sigh. "I wish I was." He points at Ig. "Those samples you are carrying will bring her back to us."

"What the hell are you talking about?"

He steps beside the tube, places a hand on it. "I can recreate her body and reconstruct her using those samples."

"You mean clone her."

"No," he shouts, shooting a glare at her. "She will still be her. Clones are a copy of the original. This will *be* her."

Despite it all, she's intrigued. "You really believe that?"

He chuckles. "I did not waste millions hunting sea monsters *not* believing this can be done. Everything is in place. All my people need are those samples."

Tears trickle down Ig's cheeks. "How are you so sure it will work?"

Murdock narrows his gaze on her. "It has been exhaustively researched by my scientists. It will work."

"More like you're hoping it will work," Ig says. "Murdock...she's gone. Let her rest now."

He slams a fist down on the small outcropping below Anna's brain and nervous system. "No! She can be brought back to me. I can have her back!"

Ig shakes her head, knowing he can see it through the nanoglass. "No. You can't. Whatever you end up creating, it won't be Anna. Even with her brain, it's immoral, and I think you know it."

He runs a hand over his slicked-back hair. "Immoral? You know what's immoral? Her love for you, you bitch!"

"So much for being civil," Ig says. "Laser."

Murdock holds his hands up, closes his eyes, and opens them again. "My apologies, Ignia I—"

"Your apologies are getting old," she says. "Just like you. Anna is dead. She loved us both. Let it be at that. Playing the Great Spirit angle isn't—"

"God, you mean."

"Whatever. Playing *your* god, will only lead to disaster. Why can't you see this?"

He doesn't say anything for a moment. Instead, he turns to look at Anna's brain.

Ig lifts her left arm, ready to kill the man. A mercy killing, really.

"Is it so wrong to want a child back?" He looks at her and tears also stream his face. "Like you want to save your mother, I want my baby girl back. That's all I want."

Her heart aches for him. And, for a minute, she almost abandons the mech. She almost gives the samples to him. Maybe he would save enough to help her mom. Her finger is hovering over the hatch release when Murdock says, "Thank you for sacrificing your mother. We all have to make sacrifices, don't we?" Gone are the tears, replaced by a thin smile.

Ig barely stops herself from opening the hatch. "What?"

"Well," Murdock says, "I can't spare an ounce of the samples. I need it all to get my Anna back."

"You injected my mom with those parasites and made her sick," Ig shouts. "You're more of a monster than the ones in the ocean!"

"So, I made an impulsive decision. I was struck with unbearable grief."

"You waited five *years* to do it! That's not impulsive. You planned it."

"So what? You led my Anna astray!" He storms toward her. "Because of you, she died!"

Ig lifts the arm with the laser canon, tears welling in her eyes and squiggling down her face. "There's only one way you can be with Anna now."

Murdock stops, eyes widening. "Ignia, I—"

Ig closes her eyes, and fires.

She doesn't open her eyes until Verity says, "Time to go, love."

Ig screams. Not from the pieces of Murdock all over the room, but by the sprawling lumps of Anna's brain, spinal cord, and nerves. If Anna wasn't truly dead before in that tube…now she is. And, perhaps, it's for the best.

If not for the mech's stabilizers, she would've fallen to her knees before the mess and whispered a prayer to Anna's remains.

Her gaze sweeps the room, taking in all the carnage.

Taking in the end of Murdock Jones.

CHAPTER 26

Two weeks later, with Anna's final remains buried, Ig kneels at Mom's bedside, holding the woman's withered, cold hand in her own.

Mom's breathing is ragged, shallow.

Bracken sits in a chair across the room, snoring.

They kept Mom at the cabin. It's where she wanted to be. On her ancestors' land. And it's on this land she wishes to return.

Tears squiggle down Ig's cheeks. Her chest burns with all the crying, but she refuses to use the inhaler. Not yet. Mom is on her back, sleeping, or unconscious, Ig isn't sure. A soft shaft of sunlight filters through the window, bathing her mom in gold. The Great Spirit, embracing Mom, comforting her during life's final breaths.

Ig kisses her mom's hand, wipes tears away, and lowers her head.

She thought she was prepared for this moment, but how could any child be prepared to confront the death of a parent? The ones who, from birth, took care of you. They guided when you couldn't quite figure something out. They scolded when you showed bad behavior. They held your hand walking through the snow and laughed with you while building crooked snowmen. They taught you how to set the bait just right on the hook before casting the line. They taught you how to change a tire and maintain a vehicle. They showed you how to plant corn and build a garden. They taught peace and love. Kindness. Compassion. Strength. They helped you grow, in other words. They made sure you learned and lived. Your parents, the only people on Earth who will never give up on you and always cheer you on.

All other love doesn't hold a candle to that of a mother's love.

And a child's love for their mother is eternal.

A hand strokes Ig's hair. "Don't give up yet, hun," Verity says.

Ig sobs, body quivering, unable to speak.

From somewhere nearby, Ash says, "Give it time."

Time…something Mom doesn't have, and yet, this all there is to cling to, except for hope.

Time…

***

"You okay?" Verity asks, pulling Ig closer.

Their gazes lock.

"Yeah. I think so."

The front door of the cabin opens, creaking on old hinges. Ig steps away from Verity, facing the open doorway.

Miles steps out…escorting Ig's mom out onto the front stoop.

Mom wobbles, squints at the bright morning sunlight…and smiles. She lifts her gaunt face toward the sun and draws in a deep breath.

Ig's hands tent over her mouth and nose, tears welling in her eyes. Her heart thuds heavily. At her side, Verity wraps an arm around her waist. Miles shoots Ig a big smile as he helps Mom along. They shuffle through the tall grasses. Mom, smiling, tears glittering her face, glances around, taking in the life she thought she lost.

This alone, seeing Mom smile with so much wonder, is all Ig needs to know everything will be okay.

Behind Miles and Mom, Bracken and Ash step through the doorway. They squint at the daylight, then smile at Mom and Ig.

Finally, Mom's eyes settle, her gaze fixed on Ig. Ig bursts out in tears, trying to simultaneously wipe the tears from her face and smile. These tears of joy.

"Hello, my dear, beautiful girl," Mom whispers and holds her arms up for an embrace.

Ig steps forward and sobs when Mom envelopes her. The year of horror is finally at an end.

In her ear, Mom says, "I love you, Ignia."

Ig hugs her mother. She buried her face into her mother's bony shoulder while Miles and Verity steadied her.

She cried. She laughed with pure joy. She held onto her Mom.

The Mother of the Sea pumps through her Mom's veins.

A total reversal, Ash had told Ig a few days ago.

She knows Mom won't regain all her strength, especially in her hands, but that's okay.

It's okay, because…

"I love you too, Mom."

The samples worked after all. At least for now.

And, for now, that's all Ig cares about.

Sometimes…the death of one, feeds the life of another.

Ig embraces her mother, and, for this moment, the rest of the world disappears.

THE END

SEVEREDPRESS

facebook.com/severedpress
twitter.com/severedpress

CHECK OUT OTHER GREAT DEEP SEA THRILLERS

LOCH NESS REVENGE
by Hunter Shea

Deep in the murky waters of Loch Ness, the creature known as Nessie has returned. Twins Natalie and Austin McQueen watched in horror as their parents were devoured by the world's most infamous lake monster. Two decades later, it's their turn to hunt the legend. But what lurks in the Loch is not what they expected. Nessie is devouring everything in and around the Loch, and it's not alone. Hell has come to the Scottish Highlands. In a fierce battle between man and monster, the world may never be the same. Praise for THEY RISE : "Outrageous, balls to the wall...made me yearn for 3D glasses and a tub of popcorn, extra butter!" – The Eyes of Madness "A fast-paced, gore-heavy splatter fest of sharksploitation." The Werd "A rocket paced horror story. I enjoyed the hell out of this book." Shotgun Logic Reviews

TERROR FROM THE DEEP
by Alex Laybourne

When deep sea seismic activity cracks open a world hidden for millions of years, terrifying leviathans of the deep are unleashed to rampage off the coast of Mexico. Trapped on an island resort, MMA fighter Troy Deane leads a small group of survivors in the fight of their lives against pre-historic beasts long thought extinct. The terror from the deep has awoken, and it will take everything they have to conquer it.

 SEVERED**PRESS**

❶ facebook.com/severedpress
❷ twitter.com/severedpress

CHECK OUT OTHER GREAT
DEEP SEA THRILLERS

MEGA
by Jake Bible

There is something in the deep. Something large. Something hungry. Something prehistoric.
And Team Grendel must find it, fight it, and kill it.
Kinsey Thorne, the first female US Navy SEAL candidate has hit rock bottom. Having washed out of the Navy, she turned to every drink and drug she could get her hands on. Until her father and cousins, all ex-Navy SEALS themselves, offer her a way back into the life: as part of a private, elite combat Team being put together to find and hunt down an impossible monster in the Indian Ocean. Kinsey has a second chance, but can she live through it?

THE BLACK
by Paul E Cooley

Under 30,000 feet of water, the exploration rig Leaguer has discovered an oil field larger than Saudi Arabia, with oil so sweet and pure, nations would go to war for the rights to it. But as the team starts drilling exploration well after exploration well in their race to claim the sweet crude, a deep rumbling beneath the ocean floor shakes them all to their core. Something has been living in the oil and it's about to give birth to the greatest threat humanity has ever seen.

"The Black" is a techno/horror-thriller that puts the horror and action of movies such as Leviathan and The Thing right into readers' hands. Ocean exploration will never be the same."

SEVEREDPRESS

 facebook.com/severedpress

 twitter.com/severedpress

CHECK OUT OTHER GREAT DEEP SEA THRILLERS

THEY RISE
by Hunter Shea

Some call them ghost sharks, the oldest and strangest looking creatures in the sea.

Marine biologist Brad Whitley has studied chimaera fish all his life. He thought he knew everything about them. He was wrong. Warming ocean temperatures free legions of prehistoric chimaera fish from their methane ice suspended animation. Now, in a corner of the Bermuda Triangle, the ocean waters run red. The 400 million year old massive killing machines know no mercy, destroying everything in their path. It will take Whitley, his climatologist ex-wife and the entire US Navy to stop them in the bloodiest battle ever seen on the high seas.

SERPENTINE
by Barry Napier

Clarkton Lake is a picturesque vacation spot located in rural Virginia, great for fishing, skiing, and wasting summer days away.

But this summer, something is different. When butchered bodies are discovered in the water and along the muddy banks of Clarkton Lake, what starts out as a typical summer on the lake quickly turns into a nightmare.

This summer, something new lives in the lake...something that was born in the darkest depths of the ocean and accidentally brought to these typically peaceful waters.

It's getting bigger, it's getting smarter...and it's always hungry.

Made in the USA
Monee, IL
24 February 2023

28572495R10104